Gold Man Review

Gold Man Review is published annually by Gold Man Publishing in Salem, Oregon.

The editors invite submissions of previously unpublished works of fiction, nonfiction, and poetry. Please find our submission guidelines and link to our submission manager at www.goldmanpublishing.com

Heather Cuthbertson
Editor-in-Chief
Heather.Cuthbertson@GoldManPublishing.com

Contents

Editor's Letter

Life is cyclical.

Last year, I was going through a lot of endings. If you read the Editor's Letter for Issue 6, you'd know that two were in fact quite significant. I lost both my parents within two months of each other. One, the day after I uploaded Issue 6 to the printer.

The idea of losing one parent was traumatizing enough, but to lose both was almost unbearable. Everything felt off. I mean, how could I live without my mom and dad, this constant presence that had been around since the beginning. At the time, I tried to console myself that there were people who lose their parents as children or never knew them at all and that I'd made it to my thirties before mine left. Only it didn't stop the hurt or the sense of being misplaced.

It still doesn't.

Just recently, I went to my brother's graduation from the Air Force's Basic Military Training. While we were out for his celebratory dinner, I glanced over at another graduate, who I could only assume was with his parents and grandparents. My brother's table consisted of a much younger demographic, namely me and his wife, her sister, my husband, and three kids. There was something sad about it to me. Another reminder of what we were missing and odd, too, that now we will have to rely on each other for guidance as we continue to navigate this world without our elders.

But with endings come new beginnings and things you never expect. The little family I have left is making positive changes and taking steps to meet the challenges of the future. But as we move further and further away from our loss, it's easy for those hard times to get brushed away and softened with time. The beauty of writing is that no matter how difficult it was to write the Editor's Letter in Issue 6, I'm grateful I did because years from now I can look back and remember how I was feeling, realize how hard it truly was, and how painful. It makes me wish I journaled more.

I've always had a problem writing emotions and I admire those who seem to describe them so effortlessly, capturing the piece that makes us human. I think it's because I spent so many years masking my feelings that they stay buried even when I want them to surface. With Issue 6, I was finally able to take a brick out of that wall and I've been so grateful for all the feedback I'd received since then. Knowing that others were listening and had experienced what I was experiencing, made me feel less alone in my grief. Because in the end, stories connect us, which is why we'll always need them, and with every story we publish, we are publishing someone's history.

This year's stories are no different. Issue 7 is full of the light and dark sides of life with a heavy dose of the unusual—something our readers have come to expect from *Gold Man*. We have work from brand new authors as well as seasoned pros represented within these pages, which made this year's issue fun to work on and develop. I'm happy with every piece we're publishing, and I hope you will be as well.

Although Issue 7 is pretty amazing in my opinion, it wouldn't have come together without the help of some new volunteers. I'd like to thank Courtney Grela, Daniel Link, Max Talley, and Abbie Waters for making Issue 7 what it is. Without you four, it wouldn't be nearly as incredible … or on time. But in all seriousness, *Gold Man Review* continues to survive in part because of all the gracious individuals who come on board year after year, so thank you all very much.

And finally, thank you to my Issue 7 contributors for submitting to *Gold Man Review* and trusting us with your work.

Here's to another year at *Gold Man*.

Sincerely,

Heather Cuthbertson
Editor-in-Chief

Gold Man Review Editors

Heather Cuthbertson
Editor-in-Chief

Nicklas Roetto
Project Editor

Courtney Grela
Assistant Editor

Daniel Link
Assistant Editor

Abbie Waters
Copy Editor

2017 Gold Man Review Readers

Michelle Modesto

Ashley Rich

Max Talley

Entangled Particles
Claire Scott

one spins clockwise
one counterclockwise
a waltz of perfection
not a missed step or
a stepped-on toe
one moves left
the other right
hundreds of miles apart
one instantly knows
the motion of the other
reacts in a flash
"spooky action at a distance"
protested Einstein
that old curmudgeon who
stated nothing can travel
faster than the speed of light

sorry Einstein
this world is spooky

what happens when one is gone
runs out of gas, collides with a comet
gets sucked into a black hole
does the other spin on senselessly
in a desolate universe
or does it disappear into dust
at exactly the same second
unable to exist alone

Miss May

Eileen Shields

"Freaks are called freaks and are treated as they are treated—in the main, abominably—because they are human beings who cause to echo, deep within us, our most profound terrors and desires." James Baldwin

You are staring. Maybe I look familiar? Maybe you wonder if we have met before? Ha! A joke. See? We have a sense of humor. That is something people don't expect. Because we are shy. All of us introverts. Perhaps that is why it took so long for the world to discover us.

To see just one of us, alone, is not so interesting. I understand if you are disappointed. But trust me, if you've seen one May, you've seen them all.

Another joke.

It seems I am all that is left. Though I've heard rumors of another in Guangdong. Still, in the time it would take to locate her … well … the writing is on the wall, isn't it? This is why I arranged this meeting. To tell our story. It is a role I am better suited to than most. You see, my father, Glenn Perlman, was a journalist, my mother, Judy, a research scientist. They were passionate about their work. It was the reason they waited so long to begin a family—too long, it turned out, hence their acquisition of me.

I honor them with this work. I believe it is why I still linger. My survival makes me unique. I have never been unique. I thought I would enjoy it more.

You will have to describe me. I ask that you be kind. The Mays whose parents told them they were beautiful suffered greatly when that reporter from the Times described our "hard, flat faces like so many identical metal folding chairs." We deserve better than such easy cruelty.

Most of what has been written about us is myth and fabrication. No wonder much of the world believes we are nothing but a hoax. Perhaps I cannot right that ship, but in the time I have left, I wish to try.

The cardboard box at your feet … do you mind? Oh, how easily you lift it! Inside you will find what little forensic documentation I've been able to collect.

Let's begin, shall we?

At the dawn of the twenty-first century, the People's Republic of China discovered it had a big problem, one of its own making.

Up till then, most of the complications engendered by the one-child law governing the nation of 1.5 billion had been predictable. But as medical science extended the lives of the elderly, forcing young couples into respectful cohabitation with parents and grandparents and often great-grandparents, even the most patient offspring grew weary of their domestic prison.

Whether a result of Western influence or simple self-preservation, the nation's youth began fleeing to jobs in distant cities to live selfish, carefree lives—or, at least, lives where, after a workday of drudgery, they could enjoy a beer in peace. Opting not to procreate at all, unwilling to doom another generation to bleak futures spent as abused nursemaids.

As a consequence, the endless stream of superfluous female children—because it's always girls who are expendable—that China had been exporting for years to the U.S. for adoption, dried to a trickle. At the same time, demand from America's infertile couples and aging couples and gay couples and philanthropic couples eager to help those less fortunate, increased. What excuse could be offered? That the fertile loins of China had embraced the narcissism of the West? In the eyes of the world, China would lose face.

While it is difficult to find much in the way of official documentation, it seems the mandate for a solution passed through the tangled intestinal tract of China's bureaucracy until it was expelled onto the desk of a low-level administrator in a sub-unit of a murky agency; the name of which loosely translates into "Intraglobal Exchange of Cultural Product." The tidy desk of my mother, Zhou Mu Li, also known as Miss May.

Through back channels and some overt bribery, I've acquired her personal journals. Their contents reveal a woman both fascinated and repulsed by the West. You see where I've earmarked relevant pages; the marginalia are my translation. Here she lambasts America's "juvenile compulsion to be the center of attention," but is amused by the nation's "bad-boy swagger."

Alongside her assignment was this list: the names of nearly one-thousand U.S. American couples who had already jumped through the great many regulatory hoops required to adopt a Chinese baby girl. Miss May's superiors did not care how the task was accomplished. Like everything else in the new China, the focus was on results. Mistakes could be Feng Shui-ed later.

I see that made you smile.

As we now know, the cloning of humans had long been possible. Unlike the U.S., China had no moral objections regarding God or the human soul, but rather recognized the country's population was already holding steady at several million more than it could handle. Resources were stretched to the limit as good citizens continued to thrive well into their "terrible burden" years.

For China, cloning was considered a parlor trick, done once or twice for show, then put away. So I imagine that when Miss May tracked down the few remaining scientists in the long neglected department of "Cellular Reproductive Genotechnology," they were thrilled to once again be of use, unpacking their centrifuges and snapping on latex gloves.

I wonder how long they debated before selecting Miss May to replicate? We can assume the choice was made from simplicity. Miss May was flattered, but her journal also reflects her fear for the physical safety of girls who, like her, would be typical dainty Chinese in a land of American Amazons.

But around the same time, a national tragedy occurred in China. These yellowed sheaves are copies of the Beijing Daily and the Nanfeng Metropolis.

Please don't remove the plastic wrap; the paper is quite brittle.

The headlines recount Chinese basketball star, Bai Zh Xiong's collapse during an important game between the Guangdong Southern Tigers and his team, the Liaoning Flying Leopards. Heart attack. He died instantly.

An autopsy was obligatory for the untimely loss of such a literal and figurative giant. It was not hard for the scientists at Cellular Reproductive Genotechnology to procure a bit of his DNA. An embryo of the two would be created—then cloned.

Which makes the man in this faded photo my father. He has a kind face, don't you think? Look at the eyes. The eye of a May has this same downturn at the corner. It is why we always appear sad.

I often imagine the moment of my conception. My mother observing through sterile goggles, warm breath fogging her surgical mask as my father's DNA is comingled with hers in a Petri dish. Her journal pages following this event are tinged with both intellectual awe and a deep well of loneliness.

I have not included them.

I'm sorry, would you mind fetching me a glass of water from the tap? Just a moment of dizziness. It will pass.

Where was I? Oh yes—the arranged adoptions could now proceed, buoyed by this inexhaustible, and relatively inexpensive supply of Mays.

America is not so big as China, but it is plenty big. After graphing the scattered towns of the adoptive families—indicated by the colored dots on this map of the U.S., it was determined unlikely that any of us would cross paths. Plus, volumes of sociological research indicated many white Americans were deeply shamed by their inability to tell one Chinese person from another. Even if they suspected, they would remain silent.

This photo, taken on the day my parents received me, is the only one I have of Miss May. There is her nose and a bit of her cheek, the rest of her hidden behind the shoulder of my father's jacket. Judy, my American mother, told me that Miss May's eyes welled with unshed tears as she handed me over. I can only imagine the agony of this childless woman forced to give away so many daughters.

The program was a massive success, until the unthinkable happened. Chinese baby girls lost their cachet. Overnight, fickle American consumers began trending toward African boys from Namibia and Liberia. The department of "Cellular Reproductive Genotechnology" began losing money, attracting government scrutiny. In response, Miss May doubled-down, tirelessly plotting strategies for marketing her girls.

This folder is bursting with her fevered manifesto of goals and objectives. But with the scientific advances in IVF and surrogacy, business went from bad to worse. The stress left her in a constant state of preoccupied anxiety until one day she lost her footing on a subway platform.

You seem incredulous. Believe me, I have turned over every stone. There is no indication of foul play. The government had no reason to fear her. She was nothing to them. However, whether there was intent on her part, we cannot know.

Here's her obituary.

No surviving family.

The irony.

Beneath China's great churning wheels of progress, the Miss May project was crushed and forgotten.

Like the original, we Mays grew up to be hard working and even-tempered. Some of our parents kept the name we were born with, although many christened their Chinese daughters Isabella or Hannah or Olivia. At one time, there were Mays living in forty-one of the forty-eight continental United States. California held over a quarter of us. There were two in Hawaii, but none in Alaska.

Our lives were unremarkable. That is, I have interviewed many

Mays who were young champions of the Spelling Bee or Science Fair, but rather than signs of genius, as their parents like all parents chose to believe, these achievements can be attributed to the fact that, like our mother, we are hopeless pleasers. This is also the reason we were popular with our teachers, but not our peers.

It was when we started high school that our mother's contingency revealed itself. Like our father, we grew very, very tall. At hundreds of schools in hundreds of towns, the *most likely to succeed* was a May. She was the star of the basketball or tennis team while simultaneously editor-in-chief of the newspaper or captain of the academic decathlon. My research shows that on more than one occasion in a championship game of one sport or another, the competing high school teams each had their own May.

But, as Miss May had predicted, no one commented on the similarity, believing it poor sportsmanship, or worse, racially insensitive. Instead our open-minded parents pointed out the razor-thin differences between Mays, which generally amounted to haircuts and jersey colors.

By the time we Mays graduated from high school, all within a year or two of each other, we excelled in every area that had nothing to do with popularity or the performing arts—having inherited our mother's tone-deafness and our father's flat feet. We were uniformly adored by our families, admired by our teachers, and shunned by our classmates.

Our adoptive parents relished the satisfaction derived from creating a success, each convinced that their support had made their May so outstanding, that their nutritious meals had made her so tall. They basked in the sunny peace of mind granted by saving a child from the backward ignorance of her home country. We were the rescue puppies who not only flourished, but went on to win best in show.

Excuse my sarcasm. But these are the facts.

I have not included many artifacts of the Mays' school days, but trust me, to visit their families is to be inundated with box after box of awards and medals and trophies, lovingly cocooned in tissue. Even after their daughters were proven to be less than exceptional—or more than exceptional, depending on your point of view—these shrines persist.

Very few Mays were lost before reaching maturity. I have records of one being killed in a freeway pileup, which also claimed the rest of her family, and another tragically contracting a deadly strain of E. coli from some bagged spinach. But the dangers of adolescence usually involve peer pressure. Mays rarely engaged with peers. The only parties I ever attended were the heavily supervised sort, where a classmate's mother forced them to include "everybody." We Mays flourished in the numbing comfort of our own protective bubbles.

Inasmuch as nearly one-thousand, overachieving, six-foot-tall Chinese girls could fly under the radar, we did. But it was only a matter of time before a confluence of Mays would lead to questions.

When it came time to apply for college, across the country, eager high school counselors breathlessly advised each of our parents that with our GPAs, extra-curriculars, and athletic ability—i.e. size—their May had an excellent shot at a top-notch school.

Perplexed admissions officers could not help but notice the sharp increase in a very narrow demographic that year—particularly since we were each encouraged to write our college essay about our adoption as a means to differentiate ourselves from other candidates and show resilience in overcoming obstacles. These colleges had no way of knowing that applicants Alexandra Kennedy and Taylor Perlmutter and Shannon Snell were virtually May, May, and May.

How many brilliant Chinese orphans could each elite university admit and still achieve balance and diversity? Harvard took five, Dartmouth took seven. My alma mater, Yale, took only three. Altogether, the eight Ivy League schools, using what I've found to be the most arbitrary of metrics, accepted sixty-seven Mays. The rest ended up at the mini-ivies, or slightly less prestigious, but still first-tier schools.

In these cloistered environments, the Mays inevitably encountered each other. Denial is a powerful thing, but in hindsight I realize I glimpsed my first sister at the Yale cafeteria salad bar. Her long hair—mine was short—pulled tight in a glossy black ponytail, revealed a familiar wide, heavy forehead and dark, sad eyes. I watched, mesmerized, as she built a tower of romaine, croutons, chickpeas, and boiled eggs, all my favorites. I was relieved when she doused it in ranch dressing. I hate ranch dressing. I put my tray down and left, purchasing my lunch at a pizza joint off campus for the remainder of the semester.

Things came to a head when as designated "student-athletes" we were expected to try out for an Olympic sport. Badminton and basketball, volleyball and water-polo, rowing and lacrosse, it seemed every team had its May. Perhaps if we had earned more medals—or any medals—the backlash that followed might have been avoided. But the only thing America hates more than a Chinese clone, is a loser.

The Mays poor performance in the 2024 Olympic games spawned many ugly rumors. I did not participate myself, but I can state unequivocally this was not a plot fashioned by a foreign nation. Rather, it was hereditary. Despite the original Miss May's drive, she did not work well with others, and we, her offspring, are lousy at the group dynamics necessary for team competition.

Even in the individual sports, like archery and fencing, we lacked a certain edge. It seems our "father," Bai Zh Xiong, was a reluctant basketball star, spending the offseason living the life of a simple farmer. In postgame interviews, he often turned the conversation from offensive strategies to the topic of his prized beets.

You think I romanticize him, but the coroner's report, here, indicates half-moons of loamy soil were found beneath his fingernails.

As the Olympics progressed, it became impossible to ignore the curiosity of nearly 10% of the female U.S. team being made up of identical, statuesque Asians. Sports journalists from around the globe pounced on the story, stalking the timid Mays who would not, in fact could not, provide any explanation. Claims of genetic tinkering drew comparisons to the steroid pumped East German swimmers of the seventies and eighties.

One enterprising reporter coerced a bitter Russian lacrosse player into collecting four separate hairs from four separate hairbrushes, securing the black threads in Ziplock bags, and sending them off to be tested. Here is a copy of the lab report. As you can see, the results were conclusive. Either one girl had used four hairbrushes or something astounding and inexplicable had occurred.

The subsequent, exhaustive, IOC investigation showed no rule violations. But while diplomatically avoiding the "C" word, their findings included one unassailable fact: eighteen years previous, within an unusually short timeframe, Americans had adopted nearly one thousand female infants from a singular, discreet Chinese government agency.

I don't need to remind you how this news exploded, complete with naysayers and doomsayers and conspiracy theorists. Old high school classmates, now slaving away in service-sector jobs, tweeted and blogged, picking at old scabs, venting that their MVP trophy had been stolen, their spot on the honor roll snatched, by "genetic freaks."

Talk show pundits, well versed in creating hysteria, sounded the call to round us up and intern us in camps. Polls were conducted, replete with pie charts and graphs, opining on exactly what, if anything, should be done about "the May problem."

Our elite universities ousted us in whatever ways they could, pulling our scholarships, claiming our presence was disruptive to campus life. I was called in front of Yale's ethics committee. They'd determined the existence of more than one of me constituted a sort of intellectual plagiarism. I packed my bags and left quietly.

Although we are ostensibly the same person, the Mays reacted to this crisis in complex and diverse ways. Many considered the discovery a betrayal of everything they'd been told about their "specialness." After all, is there anything less special than mass production? Others believed their specialness vindicated, for what could be more special than a miracle of modern science?

Like many, I initially believed the DNA tests had been intentionally or accidentally sabotaged. But as the evidence mounted, my parents encouraged me to take the long view. How I was conceived was interesting, but not imperative, to them. They taught me to view my creation objectively, without emotion or judgment. Understanding what I am became my life's work, a gift for which I can never repay them.

But I digress.

As you must remember, the Chinese government cried foul, refusing to cooperate with investigators. The internal documents I've collected show their political decision was to basically make lemonade from these lemons. A blanket invitation was extended to all the Mays. If we returned to our homeland, we would be treated with the respect and dignity accorded all native Chinese people.

By then, the nine hundred seventy-three Mays living in the United States were between nineteen and twenty-one years old, legally able to make their own decisions. Slightly fewer than half accepted China's offer. One might surmise that the Mays whose parents had pounded Chinese culture into their skulls, insuring they learn Mandarin and hosting tiresome celebrations for the year of the rat and the tiger, would be the ones who left. But in fact, that had little impact.

Glenn and Judy encouraged me to go, viewing the trip as a learning opportunity. But what most of the girls that accompanied me had in common was what I would call a lack of resilience. All of us had been over-parented, but these Mays had been so aggressively protected, they were incapable of managing their own disappointment. They clung to the fraying lifeline of propaganda; in China we would fit in, have friends, and maybe, finally, be popular.

We arrived to great fanfare: a parade of military bands and adorable pandas and colorful dragons dancing on poles. But once the Chinese officials had milked us for all the PR they could, we were relocated to a sprawling apartment complex in a desolate province. There we discovered that rather than fitting in, we were even more ostracized. Giant and foreign, our palates honed on beef and dairy, we exhibited too much eye contact, which made the natives nervous. Chinese culture lacks America's taboos regarding disparaging a stranger's appearance and everywhere we went, people scowled, "*Kow u kau*"—Mandarin for "too tall."

Those who made the journey with some naive hope of being reunited with our birth parents, soon discovered no record of our existence could be found, and our countrymen considered our obsession with individuality irritatingly Western.

As for me, all my questions were met with opposing questions, mostly about whether I'd ever been to Hollywood or had met Justin Bieber.

The Chinese government did what they could to prevent us from leaving—another face-saving issue. But with the assistance of our desperate-to-be-called-upon parents, the majority of us quietly slipped back into the United States where we gradually, blessedly faded from scrutiny.

Many of us found work in the tech sector, which granted us anonymity, and the pleasure we've always found in completing small, measurable tasks.

Of course, we all stopped using the name May.

Pleasers to the end, some Mays stoically agreed to participate in a myriad of clinical studies until they grew weary of being poked and measured. I've reviewed the reams of collected data; redundant nonsense—it proves nothing but the obvious.

Of the Mays I've spoken to over the years, the most contented seem to be those who followed our paternal tug to work the land— tending small farms and relishing the satisfaction found in cultivating perfectly identical life in carefully tilled soil.

These were also the first Mays who fell.

Just shy of our thirtieth birthday, one-by-one, hundreds of miles apart—this one in the fields, shucking an ear of corn; that one at the kitchen table, scribbling a mortgage check; another in the supermarket, sniffing the ripeness of a melon. Each felt the click, the betrayal of our father's heart—before falling like a rootless tree.

We were found crumpled over microscopes, splayed in front of open refrigerators, and slumped on city buses, dog-eared paperbacks still clutched in our hands.

This holocaust has dragged us once more into the public eye. Clickbait photos of our parents go viral—grim-lipped fathers propping up mothers, wild-eyed in grief. How can anyone who witnesses this naked anguish still question our humanity? But the comments are filled with dismissive epithets: monster, freak, clone.

My days are numbered. Even now numbness creeps into my fingers and my distant feet. Soon, I will depart this world, which I've tried but failed to please, with nothing to show for it but this cardboard box of rudimentary research, a jigsaw puzzle with missing pieces.

Do I have regrets?

I suppose I wish my life had allowed for more intimacy, more romantic love ...

Surely that cannot be a surprise? The crisis in China that led to my creation also fostered a national gender imbalance. With so few options, a strong, young man in the Yunnan Province was willing to look beyond my plain face, my enormity, my incompetence with his language. Had I known I would not get another opportunity, I might have stayed behind for him.

You blush? Ah, you wonder. Yes, physically, we Mays are the same in every way as other women. Except, of course, for our tail.

Ha!

That will be my last joke. At least it was a good one.

Tell me, do you believe in an afterlife?

It's the final question I will wrestle with. If heaven does exist, your Judeo-Christian God would surely stop me at the gates and judge me an abomination, damning me to some endless purgatory of Mays wandering the desert.

But I am at peace and ready to meet my maker. I can see her now, small and efficient, poised over a petri dish. She looks up as I arrive, and welcomes me, making a delicate notation in her notebook.

Death Rattle

Laura Schulkind

The maracas, hung crisscross over your dresser
that on rainy days you would take down, and
let me play while you danced for me,
shaking your hips.

Your mother's silver rattle,
passed to me with stories of
Cossacks shaking floorboards
while she was born below.
Teeth in Russian winters; piano keys,
clacking, each time the baby grand was hoisted
into another Lower East Side tenement.

Sifting through your button box,
your strands of beads, your lipsticks.
And the urgent rattle of dice.
How we loved games of chance!

The click and chatter of pebbles
being pulled into the sea,
as we walked the cold surf,
arms locked, heads bent to each other.
Ice in gin and tonics on the patio.

Now, the week's pills,
being arranged in ice trays,
like a game of Mancala.
A bit of juice through a straw.
The oxygen machine.

I hear it all in your last breath,
your breath that I want to breathe in and hold,
until I cannot hold it anymore.

Empathetic Selves
Alissa DeLaFuente

"Empathetic selves"—this is something I said in a workshop my team gave on cultural competence. That entire sentence, the entire experience really, blows my mind. As it was coming out of my mouth— "empathetic selves"—I thought to myself: Who am I? Who am I to be speaking to this crowd? Who am I to use those big fucking words? Who am I to be standing in front of a room of people much older and much more experienced (in all the ways) than myself, discussing anything?

My team of wonderful colleagues (again, who am I?), and I admitted that we are not experts, but that this is a conversation we want our campus to be having, so we're starting it. Grassroots kind of, I guess, but still within the middle echelons of the institution. I think we count as mid-level professionals. I have a magnetic nametag and it says "specialist."

Who am I? This is a question that I have been unable to answer to my satisfaction. I have all the pat answers down because that's the way good little girls do. I am a daughter of a self-made man who started as a migrant worker and now works as a production manager. He's Tejano, which means he's Texan, but also if you say it in Spanish it means more than just that. Much of what he knows he taught himself and learned on the job, and now he is an expert. He may not say this, but he is. My father never went to college. My family is bilingual, but I never learned Spanish because my dad was always at work. I am mixed culturally and racially. My mother is white (Anglo-European), grew up in the suburbs of California, went to college, and biked down the Pacific coast with her first husband—a man with long, blond hair and parents who didn't particularly like my mother. She is a hippie in some respects. Her second (last) husband is my father. They met working in agriculture, which is what her degree was in. I grew up in a house full of women—four older sisters with loud mouths and vibrant, stubborn personalities. Yes, I'm the baby. They all had babies except for one, so I wasn't the baby for long. None of them went to college because no one told them they could in time. Three of them were teen moms. I wasn't. One of my sisters is a cop. These are the stories I tell when people ask who I am. They tell you something, surely. They tell you who I come from, which is in a way who I am.

But it isn't everything.

"Empathetic selves" signals something else to you, or something to me, at least. It signals to me that I am somewhat highly educated—educated specifically in the realms of theory and language use—and that I believe I am speaking to highly educated peers. And this is true too. I hold an MFA in Fiction. Before that, I double-majored in English and Creative Writing and double-minored in Spanish and Education. I'm an overachiever and I work hard. I have a deep faith in education as a means of mobility and a route to financial stability, and though my belief is much more complicated and nuanced now, I still hold that belief. Where my father never set foot, here I stand. Where he would stand against the wall at the back of the room near the door if required to stay, I lead the room (with my two other teammates). What other sort of language can you expect from me? This is what comes out when I'm nervous, when I need to make sure you know that I know some things. That sort of language use is forged in the fires of grad school and an outgrowth of learning to teach English Composition by doing. My supervisors became my teaching mentors, and they were all professors of rhetoric because they were in charge of the English 101 curriculum. Things like this fell from their lips like espresso orders and yoga poses. By the first day of class I *had* to be an instructor of English Composition, so I did like good girls do, and I posed. We can call it passing, posing, mushfaking if you want to get theoretical and all code-switchy up in here. Who said, "fake it 'till you make it?" She was right.

And now, I've made it. I'm stable.

So, who am I?

I am a chameleon who doesn't really want to know exactly what people mean when they say "professional." I wear jeans all the time at work because I'm of the sneaking suspicion that the somewhat flexible and sometimes unspoken rule that jeans don't belong in a workplace stems from the old-school practice of weeding out the poor and unknowing from access to middle level professional soft-skills jobs. Jeans are for the working man—emphasis on "working," as in "out in the dirt and muck," and emphasis on "man" as in "not woman." I think my grandmother on my mom's side, who is old school in all ways but generally still sharp, would agree. She tells me I need to wear slacks. Looser slacks. She points to her pastel cotton slacks. She probably thinks I look like a foreigner and act like an alien—I'm nothing like her way of life. She asked why my boyfriend would ever marry me now that we live together and I don't know exactly what she means, but that gives you a sense of her perspective.

Being a chameleon isn't nice. I thought it would be. It's safe. It makes you safest of all, which was always my goal (I'm in therapy now that I have good health insurance, so don't worry about how much you can read into that. I'm on it). In high school, it meant all I wanted to do was blend in, which meant erasing as much as possible all the parts of myself that weren't white enough, that weren't soft enough, that weren't enough. It meant demonstrating my mastery of the English language even though I don't know any other. I cited, Lord, in my memory it is at least one-hundred bird allusions in Shakespeare's *Romeo and Juliet*. I was a master of Greek and Norse mythology and loved all things Celtic. I read *Walden*.

What about the myths, practices, and heritage from my dad's side—deeply Tejano, old Catholicism, curanderismo, and the myths and stories attached to these places, practices, and faiths? It wasn't on the menu at school, and at home I never really thought to ask. During undergrad in Tucson, I explored Mexican-American writers, Chicanos, and the culture around me, but from afar, with the distanced eye of a scholar. Now, whenever I think of claiming some story as a story related to my culture, my history, my people, I wonder who will expel me when they catch on that I'm not fitting in. Blending in doesn't work here like it did over there in my mind. Here, people assume I should know. I assume I should know, and I don't. It's much worse to be expelled by people you think of as kin than by people who you know see you as an outsider. I'd rather have the fight for entrance on the table clear as day. If I can ask the question "Will you let me in?" and "What will it take?" then someone can give me entrance, someone can show me the way.

So, back to "empathetic selves." I forget the exact context I was mentioning this in. It likely had to do with the definition of cultural competence we came up with as a group. I think I was calling back to the idea of empathy in order to reframe the conversation for all the different stakeholders in the room (should I tone it down with the in-group language already? Am I using it right?). I was trying to make the point that practicing cultural competence is really bringing our empathetic selves to work, rather than just our professional ones, because that's what we need to interact with people different from ourselves—both our students and our colleagues. I was trying to make the point that practicing cultural competence isn't something you leave at work. It's a way of being in the world—it's being kind and it's being respectful in the deepest senses of those words. It's allowing ourselves to discover that we're ignorant and then requiring ourselves to seek out knowledge. It's allowing ourselves the grace we need, in that old religious sense of the word, to keep moving.

Menopause Smith
Richard Dokey

Naomi named him Menopause because menopause was what she wanted. She did not write Menopause on the birth certificate. She wrote Cyrus. Cyrus was dreamy compared to Menopause. Cyrus was someone she had never known, but had glimpsed, late at night, when she couldn't sleep and stayed up to watch a movie with Omar Sharif or Yul Brynner. But when she spoke to Cyrus, Naomi said, "Menopause, it's time to eat" or "Menopause, don't make a mess." Menopause did not know any difference between Menopause and Cyrus. Menopause was what he heard, and Menopause came, panting, across the linoleum floor.

Naomi was cheated from the beginning. She was cheated by her father and mother, who divorced when she was three. She was cheated by Grandnanny, who took her in out of guilt. She had sex in grammar school with two boys named Emmet and Karl. In the tenth grade, she was pregnant and had an abortion during summer vacation. Done with school, Naomi took odd jobs in restaurants and behind the ticket counters of amusement parks. She married twice, divorced twice, and lived with men who came by from time-to-time, like stray dogs. None of the men loved Naomi. Naomi loved none of the men. It was a movie with John Wayne or James Arness or any man, two people of separate sex, standing in the middle of a dusty street, guns holstered, glaring at each other. One of the men was named Smith. Maybe they were all named Smith. What did it matter? Smith was only a name lined up with other Smiths in the telephone directory.

When she had to go to The Good Earth Grocery, which was just down the street, Naomi pushed Menopause in a baby carriage she found at Goodwill. People smiled when she went by. Some of them said, "What a pretty baby you have there." Others said, "My, would you look at those eyes." Naomi said nothing. She pushed Menopause into The Good Earth Grocery, got the things she needed, stuffed them in around Menopause as though he were something she had found on sale, and pushed everything home.

Naomi watched a lot of television. She read a lot of magazines. Menopause lay in his crib looking at shiny baubles and bells—which Naomi had picked up at the Dollar Store—tumble above him in the wan light. The women friends who came over to watch television with Naomi said, "Naomi, why not just put the damned thing up for adoption? There are plenty of folks who want a baby that can't have a baby. You're no fun anymore." Naomi said she'd thought about it and wasn't done thinking about it, but for now, Menopause was all right just where he was.

"He's there. I feed him. I change him. I give him a bath once in a while in the kitchen sink. As to going out," Naomi said, "what's so hot about that?"

"Why didn't you just see a doctor like before and have it taken care of?"

"I was fourteen," Naomi said.

"What's that got to do with anything?"

"I don't know what it's got to do with. I don't know why I didn't do something."

"You mean, you went ahead and had a kid, and you didn't know why you were having it?"

"I didn't know why then, and I don't know why now. Everything's pieces. What's the point here? I don't know why I didn't know why." She frowned at them. "Why not? A kid is something."

"That doesn't make any sense."

"That's how things happen. Anyway, it's something."

The women shook their heads. "Well, honey, what do you want now?"

"I don't want a thing," Naomi said.

Menopause was a tiny creature nested high up on the face of an enormous cliff. If he could have looked down, he would have been so terrified that he would never have moved. And maybe that's why Naomi kept him. There was something about Menopause that fascinated her. She felt defiant watching Menopause, on his back, helpless, dependent, without a mind to know anything about anything. There was an all-over-again about it. She studied Menopause with astonishment and confusion. Menopause was a secret. Menopause was a mystery. How could life begin and not become what life always was?

When Menopause was old enough to go to school, Naomi wrote Cyrus on all the papers. She never said Menopause to anyone but to Menopause or the three women who came over to watch television, eat Fritos, bean dip, and drink beer.

"Why do you call him Menopause then, honey?" the women wanted to know.

"It's a nickname," Naomi said. "That's all it is."

"A nickname for what?" Frieda Pruitt, who Naomi liked best,

replied. "Menopause is a queer enough name for a kid, you'll have to admit."

"My Uncle Syd called his boy Gus Spittin' Image," said Peggy Handley. "I always thought that was kind of cute, you know, because Gus is the spitting image of his old man, right down to the belly. Gus' friends call him Spitter. I call him Spitter too. Spitter has a kind of carefree ring to it, wouldn't you say?"

"You've got a kid named Cyrus you call Menopause," Wilma Inkster said. "That's one to beat, all right."

"It's just a name," Naomi said. "So what?"

"Cyrus Menopause Smith," Frieda said. "That's something, all right. You have a relative named Cyrus then?"

"I never knew any Cyrus," Naomi said.

"Where did you ever get Cyrus?" Peggy said. "Cyrus and Menopause together? Now that is something."

"It's just a name in a movie I saw on television. It was about some Greeks and some Persians, I think. Anyway, it had Charleton Heston."

"I like Charleton Heston," Wilma said. "I didn't know there was any Charleton Heston movie about Greeks and Persians. Maybe you were thinking of *Ben Hur*."

"It might not have been Charleton Heston," Naomi said. "What difference does it make? I never heard any Cyrus before and I liked Cyrus."

"I never heard of any Menopause before," Peggy said. "And I wouldn't like being called that."

"So," Naomi said, "you don't have a problem then, do you? He's only Menopause around here."

"Well, he is your kid," Peggy said.

"Yes, he is," said Naomi. "He's my kid."

"I like Cyrus myself," said Freida. "It's different. You'd probably never ever meet any real Cyrus' in your whole life."

"You'd never meet any Menopauses either," said Wilma. "That's for damned sure."

"He's only Menopause here," Naomi said, and switched on the television.

One day in the first grade Billy Stapleton said, "Hey, you, Menopause."

Menopause turned around and said, "What?"

"You see," Billy said to Arnie Farmer and Hank Nestor, who were standing around.

"Hey, Menopause," Hank said. "Really?"

Arnie said, "Menopause! Menopause! Menopause!"

They laughed and skipped away.

When he got home, Menopause asked, "What's my name?"

"What do you mean, what's your name?" said Naomi.

"Billy Stapleton called me Menopause today."

Naomi thought of Frieda, Wilma and Peggy. "Listen. Your name is Cyrus Menopause Smith."

"You only say Menopause."

"It's a nickname. A nickname is no big deal."

"Why don't you call me Cyrus?"

"I just said Cyrus."

"You always say Menopause. Everyone at school says Cyrus. I have two names?"

"Everybody has two names, a real name and a kind of other name. You're Cyrus and Menopause at the same time. There's no big deal about it."

"I don't know," Menopause said. "They laughed."

"Maybe I should never have said Menopause, but I said it, and now, so what? A name is all it is."

"What if I don't want to be called Menopause? What if I just want to be called Cyrus?"

"Okay," she said. "You're Cyrus out there and you're Menopause around here. How's that?"

"I don't like Menopause. I don't know anybody else named Menopause."

"You don't know anybody named Cyrus, do you?"

"No," Menopause said.

"You see? It's just a name. No matter what you're called, there you are. Right? Now get your ass in the bathroom. Wash your hands and face. Go on. Dinner's ready."

Next day at school everyone said Menopause. Menopause cried. When Menopause told Naomi about it, she felt a twinge. It was all right with Menopause on the floor playing with his trucks and blocks, all right putting him to bed so she could stay up to watch *Lawrence of Arabia* or *Mogambo* with Clark Gable and Ava Gardner, or to read the magazines she wanted to read. Why was it anyone's business? School had never given her a damned thing.

Frieda and Peggy and Wilma had stepped in it. Now she had to clean up something she didn't have to clean up before. She had no particular feeling about Menopause. Menopause was something she brought home that could have been put to sleep. Naomi lived with Menopause. She took care of Menopause. And what was all this about going out to have fun? Still, once a week, the women came over to drink beer, eat Fritos and bean dip and watch television with Naomi, while Menopause Smith lay asleep in the next room.

When Menopause came home crying, Naomi felt everything that was after her, was after her again. That made a new ambivalence about Menopause. Something was at the door and she couldn't keep it out. Kids asked their mothers, "What's menopause?" The mothers called school and said they didn't want their children having anything to do with anyone with a name like that.

This frightened and angered Naomi. When she thought about Menopause, she thought about slapping him. Then she thought about tucking Menopause into bed. She thought about throwing Menopause into the street. Then she thought of Menopause on the floor with his blocks and trucks while she nailed the door shut. She thought about telling Menopause to fix his own crap to eat. Then she thought about making Menopause an angel food cake with peppermint cream cheese frosting, which was his favorite. Sometimes, when Menopause was at school, she wanted to pack her things. When Menopause came home, she wanted to chain him to the wall.

Frieda and Peggy and Wilma noticed the difference.

"Don't you see, honey?" Frieda said. "It's not working for either of you."

"As plain as the nose on your face," Peggy said. "Nobody's happy here."

Naomi looked blankly from one to the other. "Get out!" she said.

"No, no," Frieda said. "Come on now, honey, we're your friends. The older he'll get, the worse it'll get. As plain as your nose."

"It's not worth it," Wilma said. "What are you getting out of it, who never wanted to be tied down?"

"Naomi," Peggy said, "The kid deserves better. None of it is his doing, you know."

"It's my fault," Naomi said, "Is that what you're telling me?"

"Fault? No one's talking about any fault," Frieda said. "It is what it is. But we can't just sit around and say nothing. We're your friends. Put the kid up for adoption. That's the right thing to do."

"I won't give away what's mine," Naomi said. "He's mine, whether I want him or not."

"Sure. He's yours," said Wilma. "That's not the point. What about him? Have you ever thought of foster care? I heard it's a kind of trial thing. It lets you see what's what to see."

"What do you mean trial?"

"It's too damned much around here, just him and you. How can you think? You need space to think. You can see that," Wilma said.

"I can think with him right here," Naomi said. "Why can't I?"

"No, you can't," Wilma said. "How can you think when you don't know what to think about. You just go on not thinking."

"That's true," Frieda said. "That's how I was with Ed before we split."

"I don't know what to think, you mean."

"There you are," Frieda said. "You need space to find some balance. You need space to figure it out. Wait too long, you won't be able to figure out anything and then where will you be?"

"What do you mean by that?" Naomi asked.

Frieda shrugged. "Honey, isn't that how it is?"

So Naomi put Menopause into a foster home.

The people were a Mr. and Mrs. Charles Henninger. Naomi did not want to meet any Mr. and Mrs. Charles Henninger. The woman at The Children's Center showed Naomi a photograph. Naomi set the photograph on the desk. They were like other Mr. and Mrs. Charles Henningers Naomi had seen over the years. They said they wanted to put Menopause into a new school across town.

Naomi wanted to ask, sometimes, would she ever see Menopause? Then she didn't want to see Menopause. She packed the few things Menopause had and carried them to the front door. She gave them to Mr. and Mrs. Henninger. Naomi wanted to say goodbye to Menopause, but she couldn't say goodbye. She could say, I'll see you later, Menopause, but that sounded odd. She stood at the door watching Mr. and Mrs. Charles Henninger and Menopause get into the black sedan. Menopause looked at Naomi from the rear seat. Naomi thought she could wave, but she didn't wave. Menopause looked at Naomi through the window, turning his head so that he could look until the sedan went around the corner. Naomi closed the door, sat down in the living room, and switched on the television.

Naomi lost two jobs, found two more, and then settled in as a manager for the All-Star Laundromat across from The Good Earth Grocery. She thought about Menopause and wondered about him. She asked the woman at The Children's Center about seeing Menopause sometime, nothing big, just to see him maybe and to see what he was doing. The woman said to give it time. It wasn't a good idea to bounce Menopause around like a rubber ball. So Naomi thought, what the hell, and went out with Frieda and Peggy and Wilma.

After a while Naomi felt something inside like a sponge going dry on the kitchen sink. She went to where Menopause lived to see what she could see. She stood across the street in the shadow of an oak tree, wondering about Menopause. The black sedan pulled up. Mr. and Mrs. Charles Henninger got out. Then Menopause stood on the sidewalk looking at Naomi, who came out from under the tree. Menopause said something to Mr. and Mrs. Charles Henninger. He walked across the street. Mr. and Mrs. Charles Henninger pretended to be talking about their front yard. Menopause was almost as tall as Naomi was tall.

"Hello, Mother," Menopause said.

"You never call me that," Naomi said.

"You're my mother," he said.

"I know I am," Naomi said. "Anyway, then, hello, Cyrus. I guess you're Cyrus now all the time."

"And I'm going to be Henninger too," Menopause said.

"Henninger," Naomi whispered.

"Cyrus Henninger," Menopause said. "I can be Cyrus Henninger and it won't make any difference. Isn't that so, Mother?"

Naomi stood in the hot light staring at her son. With more understanding of language than she cared to admit, Naomi realized that what had always came for her, had come for her again.

Renting My Body
Toni La Ree Bennett

I believe the same hour on different days is
　　　　not the same but nothing can change
　　　　its three o' clockness.

My daily delusion —
expecting the same old sun to rise
　　　　on a different world.

And while admitting that the sun,
　　　　topography as variable as a Vegas roulette table,
　　　　could no more become a moon than I could,

I still believe the right hairstyle can affect my destiny.

But while I sit on the border
　　　　between reinvention and recycling,
　　　　a vision, surpassing any desert revelation, detonates:

I am in my own skin
　　　　and in no other —
　　　　when all along I thought I was only
　　　　renting my body.

Pretty Shoes with Tassels

Simar Malhotra

You have to meet the boy and his family. The *panditji* deems your match astrologically harmonious. The date, day and time of his and your birth are appropriate for your matrimonial union. Your interests and his? Not sure. Your values and his? Not sure either.

Your mother stresses over the appropriateness of the number of pleats in your *sari*. The first impression must be the best impression. Maybe the extra five pleats add too much volume. That may make you come across as a painted woman. No, the oddity lay in the yellowness of the *sari*. You change and wear your older sister's pink one. Your mother tells you not to wear red lipstick; that's too bold. Only a slight tinge of rouge to the cheeks. A tinge is a tinge.

You go downstairs. Your mother ushers you into the kitchen. They are coming soon; you are to prepare tea. The tea has to be good; its taste will dictate whether there would be a follow-up meeting and define whether you are truly worthy of the boy or not. Because the skill of adding tea leaves, sugar, and milk to boiling water is an irrefutable determiner of your character, compatibility, and intellect. Your mother has already taken out her fanciest china. The one she refused to let you use when your boss came over for dinner. She has turned on the AC in the drawing room and arranged the cushions and the photo frames. The frames today only adorn your pictures. There are some from your older sister's wedding, but she's not in any of them. Others are from the day of your graduation and award ceremonies. You're disgusted at the ostentation. But she's your mother and you have to love her and all her actions because *they are always in your best interest*. The chandelier is turned on. The curtains are drawn back. You see your dog napping outside on the grass that's been recently planted. In the plants that line up at the back of the garden, you spot a single yellow flower. As you gaze into the flower, you see the greenness fade away. Soon, you're staring too hard, focusing all visionary energy on that yellow flower. You see black and red vortex rings swimming around as all forms and figures wane. You sense your eyes strain until they start to water. Your dog sits up, startling you. You look away and retreat into the kitchen.

The bell rings. Instrumental "Jingle Bells" blares through the small speaker that notifies the house of a visitor. You're embarrassed at the sound. Your older sister, Sarika, hated the ringtone, you hate the ringtone, and your younger sister doesn't seem fond of it either. But it's still been ringing, every day, no one bothering to change it. You instinctively head towards the door. Your mother stops you and points towards the kitchen. You must wait.

"Don't come out until I tell you to," she says. "Taste the tea before serving." You know what she means is *don't flub it up*. You are twenty-four-years-old and you should want this match to work out as much as she does. She looks at you intently, taking you in: your face, your hair, your attire. Before leaving the kitchen, with her finger, she dots the back of your ear with black kohl that is lining her eyes. It's for good luck, to prevent evil spirits from nearing you. You suddenly recognize how real this is. You shiver even though it's June.

You hear your father open the door and greet them. You cringe to hear his voice dripping with blandishment. Your mother joins him and welcomes them into the house. You try to peep covertly from behind the kitchen door. Your younger sister smacks you, gesturing with her eyes to concentrate on simmering the tea. She's helping you in its preparation instead of studying for her high school exams. You've never been culinarily adept. You wonder if she's thinking about your older sister in that moment. She acquired all her epicurean skills from her.

You hear soft chit-chatting through the kitchen door. You strain your ears to get a murmur of what's happening. There seems to be three, no, four people. Your mother comes and tells your younger sister to carry water outside. The smile on your mother's face dies out in a jiffy and her serious, anxiety-ridden one resurfaces. She eyes you and untucks a strand of your hair from behind your ear. She examines you from head to toe another time, now frustrating you with her pedantry. This is your cue too. You pour the tea in the cups, arrange the cups in the tray, and wait to carry the tray into the living room. You must perform well.

Your sister returns; it's your turn now. She winks at you and nods in approval. She likes the look of the boy. That's a good start. You're almost excited but you remember what your older sister told you a few months into her marriage: Hide till you can. Be invisible. Bend. Lay. Crouch. Bow. Anything to last longer. Be boring. Be somber and submissive and subdued. Smile. Only a little. Don't show your teeth. Make small talk. If asked.

You take a deep breath, nod at your younger sister, and go to the living room. The moment you enter everyone pauses conversation and looks at you. You gulp. You hate being under the spotlight. All the world doesn't have to be a fucking stage all the time, you think.

You stretch your lips awkwardly. You hope it can be read as a smile. You try not to straight up eyeball the boy. He's almost good looking. He's got dark, soft-looking hair, fair skin, a short, almost inviting stubble, clean fingernails, and expensive cufflinks. He shouldn't be like your older sister's man, you wishfully think. He'll probably care for you like he seems to care for himself. Salon appointments and the like.

You observe the rest of the guests. He's come with his mother, father, and sister. The sister is younger than him and beams brightly at you. You immediately feel lighter and release your breath. You place the tray on the table and take a seat across from the boy's family. The mother and father return your *namaskar*, the boy nods kindly at you in acknowledgment.

As you sit silently, aware of all your actions being inspected, you wince inside. You know each twitch of your muscle, every micro-movement of your body is watched closely, conspicuously. You think maybe you should have told your father about Sarika's man. About what her man used to do to her. Maybe things could have ended differently. Maybe things could have ended with her alive. Maybe you wouldn't have had to fake this family of four. Maybe you wouldn't have been forced into marrying a stranger too. Or maybe it wouldn't have made a difference. Maybe guising Sarika's miscarriage as accidental was okay. Maybe your mother, who still continues to overlook the truth, is right in doing so. Maybe not telling your father or anyone else did save, in a messed-up world, the family name. Maybe you could tell your father now. About the lies and the beatings, the fights, and the molestation. About Sarika's three a.m. silent phone calls whose conversations consisted of nothing but her pounding heart and shallow breathing for tears would be too loud. About her man's abrupt change. About that accidental miscarriage which was not an accident. Maybe he did know. Maybe he, too, condoned it with silence like your mother.

Maybe you should stop thinking about such things.

Even after you place the tea tray on the table, no one gets up to take it. They wait to be served. You are supposed to serve, you realize. Everyone drinks the first sip in silence. You're surprised to feel your heart beat faster. You're anxious. You want them to like the tea even though you want nothing more to do with them.

The boy's father says that it's in perfect accordance with his taste. You bless your younger sister in your mind. You watch your mother's lit face. You know that she is already foreseeing the wedding festivities. You did well. She's happy. She's happy after a long time.

"Rhea cooks very well," she says, "despite being a working woman. You should try her *aate ka halwa*. It's mouth-watering."

You try to appear shy and look down at your folded hands in your lap, fervently curbing your urge to tell your mother not to lie. The elders continue to talk. About weather and work and politics, anything, surreptitiously trying to verify the information *panditji* provided the two families with.

"Have you known *panditji* for a long time?" the boy's father asks your father.

"Yes, it has been many years," your father answers. "He has made lots of matches in our family. Someone I can blindly trust."

Yes, so blindly that he blinds you, you think.

"So, you have a logistics business, right?" the boy's father asks. "My cousin is also in that industry. Garvit Anand, you wouldn't know of him, would you?"

"No, the name doesn't ring a bell. It's quite an expanding industry today. Many new entrants are crowding it. Especially with Modi's new governance and the GST, you know."

"Oh, you're quite right. So, have you all always lived in Delhi or ..."

"My wife and I shifted from Lucknow after ... uh, right before Rhea was born," your father responds. He doesn't say after your older sister was born.

You stare into your cup of tea; you want to block out this irrelevant chit-chat. You think of you. You shouldn't make conversation with the man you may end up marrying in the next few months. That will make you more visible. And you have to be invisible, your older sister said. You feel him watch you. You try to sneak a glance of him while sipping the tea as inconspicuously as you can manage. You see him do the same. There is a frisson. You avert your gaze immediately, ashamed and embarrassed. You see him smile and continuing to look on unabashed. You want to play the game too, but you must be somber, submissive and subdued. As you look down, you notice his shoes. They're pretty shoes, shoes with tassels. Tassels, especially on shoes, have always fascinated you. But in a dark, eerie sort of way, like a foreboding. Your younger sister always thought there was something evil about tassels. Now you're annoyed at her for making you think this way. You don't want to think of tassels as evil. You want to like tassels. It's easier that way.

Both pairs of parents address the boy and you. They look satisfied with each other. It means that they like each other. It means that the marriage is happening. Your father's smile is less broad than everyone else's. It means that he has to bear the entire cost of all the wedding celebrations. Again.

"You can show Abhimanyu around the house, Rhea," your mother says with caution in her eyes and hiding excitement behind a reservation in her tone. That's your cue for act two.

He stands as you stand and straightens his coat and shakes his wristwatch. You walk him around the first floor.

You speak minimally, in short sentences. Despite yourself, Sarika's instructions play in the background. "That's the kitchen. That's the TV room. Outside is the garden."

"It's a very pretty house," he says. "The interiors are decorated so tastefully. Have you travelled around a lot?" He looks at the elaborate Egyptian masks hung on one of the walls.

Sarika had brought them when she visited Egypt on a trip.

"No," you say. "Those were a gift."

You feel tense; the masks always make you nervous.

"I could show you upstairs," you say, already pointing towards the staircase.

You walk one step behind him even though you're leading. As you walk, you notice his gait. It's confident but not in an imposing, condescending sort of way. Even as he walks in front of you, he walks front-beside you. That's a good thing, you think. Maybe for once the *panditji* did a fine job at matchmaking. Or maybe the boy just didn't know where to go. You like to think the former.

You continue upstairs. "This is my parent's room. This is the prayer room. This is the guest room." You smile at the end of each statement so as not to seem rude.

"This is my bedroom. I share it with my younger sister. There is a balcony inside."

You walk him into your room. He looks around—at the picture frames and the paintings hung on the wall. They are mostly of you and your younger sister and both of your friends. There's one with Sarika but you don't mention her. This is what your mother's cautionary glace was about. You are a regular family of four, not a family of four and a dead girl.

He admires the paintings and asks if you've done them. You unsuccessfully stifle your laugh at "done them." He stares back un-humored.

"I ... Yes, I have," you say and walk to the balcony.

You two gaze at the road. There are cars and scooters parked, dogs running about. The breeze makes your *sari* flutter. You know he is appraising you. You feel conscious but you don't dislike the appraisal.

You're glad your mother pulled out that strand of hair. To ease yourself, you consider it a partition between you two.

"So," he says.

"So," you say.

"So, what do you like to do for fun?"

You're confused by his question. It is more than a yes-and-no question. It is an open-ended question. It is a real question. Sarika always said it would never be about you, that you should never try to make it about you, that you must ensure it's never about you. But this *was* about you. And you like things being about you. *What do you like to do for fun?* Maybe it's a trick question. You want to say your job. Your job because it gets you money and the independence and self-sufficiency are magnetic. Because it's helped you grow as a person and there is no more pleasure than in knowing you've helped someone up the professional ladder. Because you genuinely think it's fun.

"I like to cook, paint and sing," you say, mechanically. Even though your younger sister bangs at the bathroom door when you croon in the shower.

"That's great. You'll love my sister. She's likes to sing too. She's trained in Carnatic music, in fact."

You smile and nod. You show your teeth a little bit this time. He's growing on you. He must be a loving brother. He must also be culturally aware to know about the different types of classical music.

"Is there a certain kind of music you like to sing?" he asks.

You hesitate. You're caught off guard again. You want to say pop. You want to say Beyoncé and dance-y *Punjabi* music.

"I like Indian folk music," you say. *Punjabi* music could be folk music, couldn't it?

"Aunty mentioned something about your work?" he asks again.

You're astounded now. Happy astounded. He calls your mother aunty. He's asking about your work. He either read your biodata thoroughly or paid full attention to your mother. Both mean he's great. Fucking tassels don't mean anything. He isn't like Sarika's man at all. He couldn't be posing so many trick questions. You think it's okay to drop the façade now. You don't have to continue to be somber, submissive, and subdued.

"I'm an HR consultant. I help people get jobs by connecting job-seekers and organizations with vacancies. I quite like it, the work, even though it takes up a lot of my day."

"That's interesting."

No one at home really understands your obsession with your work. You're excited that the man you may end up marrying in the next few months is interested in your work.

You go on, unthinkingly. "In fact, I got a message in the morning saying they're promoting me to Director at the Delhi branch."

His face visibly drops. He's not wearing the smile he was while talking about Carnatic music. You think something is wrong. Maybe you shouldn't have said the director part. No one likes a show-off.

"Good," he says, curtly. "It'll be difficult to balance everything after getting married though, right? With all the household chores and all. You should just help with my sister's music practices, you know, and leave the rest to me." Then he adds with a pause and the most ill-intentioned smile. "Let me care for you."

You're hit right in the face.

You stare at him. You stare hard and you're not somber, submissive, or subdued about it. The breeze becomes stronger and blows into your face, loosening your hair. You shake your head. You're not going to be another Sarika, you decide. You decide that you're not going to be invisible because you like visibility. You don't want to lay or bend or crouch or bow.

"Right," you say, taking in what he just said. You laugh. It's not a pleasant laugh. It's an I-told-you-so laugh, I-so-fucking-told-you-so.

You see his eyes bug out in surprise, squint in confusion, and then his eyebrows furrow in fury. You continue. You laugh boisterously and brusquely, the echoes ringing in your ears, his ears.

You hear your mother call you downstairs. Both of you walk back in silence. You don't walk behind him this time; you walk a step in-front. You see opened boxes of Indian sweetmeats. You're officially bride-to-be. Maybe that kohl didn't help much. Your decisions of visibility and invisibility don't matter. Because decisions are never going to be yours to take anymore. Those tassels, those fucking tantalizing tassels, you think. Maybe Sarika felt the same way. Trapped.

Night Watch

Kathleen Tyler

who could bear to not watch
them sleep pale—

faced girls blue roses in fists

yesterday sets itself into motion
each of its syllables a flower

closing

a painting is just another surface
         there were hundreds I hear

strolling around representation   its formal gardens

petal by petal the subject

disappears

who will stroke their hands
their hair?

Long Enough to Watch the Trees Emerge

Patty Somlo

Fog rises, revealing a ragged line of Redwood trees. Above is white, thick, and impenetrable. But below, at the edges, wisps float in air and when I'm not looking, vanish.

A favorite game of mine is to sit here long enough to watch the trees emerge. The beauty of conifers, tall, dark and green, unwrapped like Christmas gifts from the fog, makes my heart knock. It doesn't matter how many times I've done it before.

I've come here for vacation, flying into Oakland and driving north. For years, I lived in San Francisco, only a short distance south. If I'd wanted, I could have come for the day. But I prefer to sleep in the quiet next to the river and wake up with fog clinging to the trees.

A decade ago, I moved to Oregon, where creeks run wild and wide, making this river look like the consequence of someone having left the faucet on too long. Yet there's something so special about this place. I'm trying to figure it out now.

The cabin's wooden deck has started to rot from the rain. It's chilly because of the fog, so I've put on my sweatshirt and jacket to sit outside. Everywhere I look, I see birds: jays, crows and robins. Yesterday morning when my husband Richard was here, a hummingbird hovered at eye level in front of us, showing off.

Richard and I first came here before we were married. Typical for San Francisco where we lived at the time, the morning was windy and socked in with fog. We ate breakfast at a crowded café, both of us feeling low from the gray day.

"Let's go for a drive," Richard suggested as we stepped out onto the sidewalk, pushing past the crowd waiting to get inside.

About ten miles north of San Francisco, the fog disappeared. By the time we reached Guerneville on the Russian River, the temperature had hit eighty. Women walking on the sidewalks were dressed in halter tops and shorts. I felt hot and foolish in my turtleneck sweater and jeans. I bought a pair of shorts and a pale blue tank top in a shop on River Road, then ducked into the ladies' room at Pat's Café next door and changed.

The promise of sun drew us here over and over again. San Francisco is a city without summers. Tourists who visit in July and August don't know this. On July afternoons, the visitors can be spotted shivering in their shorts as the fog blows across the Golden Gate Bridge. After years of never leaving my San Francisco apartment without a coat, hot summer days here at the Russian River seemed magical, the way stepping out of the Honolulu airport feels in December.

We stayed first on Fourth of July weekend, in a room with a deck overlooking the river. By that time of year, the river had warmed enough for swimming. We got up early on Saturday morning and drove upstream. At a dark spot in the woods, we launched our canoe, packed with turkey and avocado sandwiches, two cold peaches, and several bottles of orange soda.

Richard sat in the back directing. We ran into rocks and occasionally slid up against the bank, argued and laughed. Sunlight sparkled across the river, drenched emerald by the reflection of the trees. Midway down the river with the sun overhead, we dragged the canoe onto a small sandy beach. Starved from paddling, we devoured our sandwiches, which tasted far more wonderful than sliced turkey on whole wheat bread ought to. Richard told me about the girl he'd fallen in love with when he was sixteen and working as a summer camp counselor and about the hayride they went on the night they first kissed.

After that weekend, Richard and I kept coming back. I created little rituals, the way families probably do that rent the same summer cabin each year. My favorite was to get up early and sit by myself on the deck. I'd sip dark roast coffee and write as I watched the fog stretch and thin, seducing me with occasional peeks at the trees. If I was lucky, an osprey would soar past. Nearly every morning, I got to see great blue herons and ducks.

My father rarely sat outdoors. I grew up believing him to be allergic to the sun and this was one reason our family never sat together on sandy beaches or drifted down sun-dappled rivers in boats. Being a military family, we spent every summer moving.

On our drives across country, we stopped at all the tourist spots—Disneyland and Knott's Berry Farm, Carlsbad Caverns, the Painted Desert, and the Grand Canyon, of course. I don't recall ever sitting alongside a river or stream. My father's lack of interest in the outdoors may have stemmed from the fact that he was a city boy. Born and raised in Cleveland, as my mother had been, my father drove us to his home city every July. On those sweltering, humid afternoons, we would sit inside one of my relatives' hot, old row houses, playing endless games of Monopoly and cards.

Over the years, near the military bases and small towns where we lived, I discovered pieces of nature and learned to enjoy them on my own. At a cabin on Oahu's Windward Coast, where we stayed with families of my parents' friends renting the neighboring cabins, I bodysurfed the huge waves while my mom and dad sat inside. It was an isolated, windswept beach with nothing but the sound of crashing waves and a long stretch of sand, dotted with a handful of worn wooden cabins.

When we left Hawaii, we moved to a small Southern New Jersey town. Sometimes, I'd go off and play by myself on the Mount, a tree-covered hill that had served some part in the Revolutionary War. There weren't any rivers or creeks, but at least our little hilltop had woods. I loved hiking up to the top, listening to the crunch of dry leaves under my boots.

The town of Monte Rio where Richard and I are staying along the Russian River is a throwback to another time. A Quonset hut houses the movie theater. Hand-painted posters for Alfred Hitchcock's *The Birds* and the James Dean classic, *Rebel Without a Cause*, grace the outside metal walls. Every Fourth of July, families gather on the beach for the annual water parade. Local businesses and families tie canoes together to construct floats that meander downstream. At the end of the parade, the volunteer fire department shoots water out of fire hoses from trucks parked on the bridge. A crackling sound system blasts out John Phillip Sousa as the water turns red, white, and blue. Then, as the air fills with the familiar strains of the national anthem, everyone gets up from their lawn chairs and sings.

The parade announcer will sometimes note that a family has been vacationing at the river for decades. When I hear this, or see the moms, dads, kids, and cousins canoeing together or gathered on the sand, I feel sad. It takes growing older to know what you've missed. Today, I find myself wondering how it might feel to share the memory of fun times here over the years instead of cherishing my solitary relationship with the river, the fog, the birds, and the trees.

I wasn't aware as a child that I substituted relationships with places for close, long-lasting connections with family and friends. All the moving around caused me to try and anchor myself in a place. In Hawaii, I had the wild Pacific Ocean and the green volcanic hillsides of the Pali we drove up and down on our way to the Windward Coast. There were also flowers growing in our yard—bright hibiscus next to the tan wood roses. And the yellow-white, intoxicatingly fragrant plumeria that I strung into leis, alternated with lavender orchids.

In New Jersey, I had trees and Woolman's Lake, which froze solid after Thanksgiving for ice skating. Later, when we lived in a second-floor apartment near Frankfurt, I rode my bike through the woods on a path that connected small, scattered German towns.

Only as I've gotten older have I realized that most of my interactions with people are strained. I've tried to change, but I still slip into my childhood role of being the new kid in school, the one always trying to please. I wonder if people sense the desperation I feel, the terror I had growing up that I'd never make a single friend, and this causes them to back away. It's easier to sit and watch the trees. I feel certain that nature won't reject me.

Richard and I thought we'd be coming here for weekends and occasional week-long stays for decades. But like many San Franciscans, we woke up one day and discovered that San Francisco had become a city we could no longer afford. Confident that all the moving around would make it easy for me to settle into a new place, I wrapped our dishes in sheets of newspaper, and watched the movers carry our carefully-labeled cartons out to the van.

The move to Oregon was not as easy as I'd expected. I didn't realize what I'd been missing until I came back here. That's when I understood that this place had become a kind of home.

Over the years, we became friends with Don and Rick, the previous owners of this place. Don hung stockings filled with candy over the cabin's fireplace one Christmas Richard and I came to stay. We'd been feeling low, not being close enough to our families to celebrate the holiday with them and having no children of our own. That simple gesture made us feel as if we weren't alone.

On Christmas morning, we woke to sunshine and frost on the trees out front. Initially, it was too cold for me to sit outside, so I carried my coffee to the rocking chair and slid the chair over to face the window. At that moment, sunlight hit the frosty leaves, causing the entire tree to shimmer.

I used to like coming back after the winter and seeing how the river had changed. Some years, the beach at the bottom of the hill emerged and you could sit there in plastic chairs and let your mind sail west toward the Pacific as you watched the river gently flow down. You could count on broods of baby ducks, swimming like little yellow thumbs behind their moms, and once in a while, recklessly scampering onto the bank. We liked to rattle potato chip bags and watch mom and her brood waddle up and wait, their beaks pointed toward our hands.

In the golden hour before sunset, the light would hit the old hotel sign on the opposite shore, causing an unexplainable sense of yearning to well up in my chest. I may have tried in this place to capture a childhood I'd not been lucky enough to have. As I sit here now, years after that first visit wondering if I'd come back, I understand that what I lost in life can never be replaced.

Don and Rick retired to the desert and the cabin is managed by a vacation rental company. The plants, once nurtured by Rick, who also tended the glorious garden that spills down the hill, have died. There are, I've come to see, rivers in Oregon more magnificent than this, wild and scenic streams whose rushing currents awaken places this quiet river can't touch in me. I see now that I've begun the process of drifting away. But while my right foot has stepped into Oregon, my left foot is still here, waiting to lift and let me continue on my way.

Hog's Breath Saloon: Raw Bar Cam
Bob Zahniser

http://www.resortcams.com/webcams/hogs-breath-raw-bar/

Sometimes it's just the sounds of someone
out of sight
then suddenly visible
                              pushing a broom
through the empty bar.

Others
it's people drinking and dancing
while you flip the stream to full screen
and guess
who's going to get laid.

The band's vocals are clear
but the drinkers, lovers,
hopeful strangers
murmur just beyond the edge of comprehension
except for the occasional snatch
amidst the mutter.

But the hand brushing hair away from another's face
the boisterous dancers
   rotating buttocks to crotch
the momentary sadness
   in the glance
of someone watching another
                              walk away
speak of a longing
      an escape from loneliness
            a surrender to the moment
in a way that you
      alone in an empty room
      watching your laptop

cannot.

The First Time I Dropped Acid

Ken Mootz

The first time I dropped acid I'm at the Van Halen concert and I like, you know, don't know what I'm doing until I'm doing it, and my buddy keeps telling me to "lick this stamp, lick this stamp" and I tell him to quit harshin' me 'cause I'm listening to Eddie's guitar solo and wishing that I am the guitar strings that Eddie's strummin' but my buddy tells me this is an extra special stamp that isn't sold at the post office, and that's when I know that maybe there is some sort of power, like chocolate or cinnamon or acid on this stamp and like, I've heard great things about acid, like, how it makes you stronger and better and faster, and everything is better on acid, especially life, and I've always wanted to try acid, just like, you know, I've always wanted to bungee jump or parachute or run naked through a crowded shopping mall, but I've always been scared, always scared, always-always-always-always scared, never taking a chance and like, you know, going all the way and taking the plunge deep into the ocean of acidy goodness, so I lick the stamp, and man, I lick that stamp like it has never been licked, I lick it up good, real good, really-really-really good, and I'm waiting for the power to flow through my veins and turn me into a superhero, and I wait and wait and wait, and nothing happens, and I begin to think that maybe I have a defective stamp, and maybe I only licked a real stamp from the damn post office, and then … WHOA-whoa-whoa-whoa-whoa-WHOA, I'm getting hot, my forehead-chest-legs-arms, I mean really-really-really hot, every inch of me is steaming hot, and then I look at my clothes and they're on FIRE, I can't believe it, I don't feel nothing and I can't smell smoke, but I'M ON FIRE, dude, and wow, that isn't cool, no, that's about as opposite to cool as opposite gets, so I rip off my shirt and tear off my pants and underwear and socks and I'm free at last from the fire of hell, and I feel good, I feel real good, I feel so good I feel like eight hundred bucks that's how good I feel, and I feel like I can fly, I can feel the wings sprouting from my shoulders, so I keep jumping up and down so I can take off and fly above the crowd and turn them on just like I've been turned on, but I can't fly, no, I can't get off the ground at all, the demons behind me have their hands on me and are holding me down cause I am in their way, I am in their way, well, screw them, screw the servants of the man, the man has kept me down long enough, the man always has to have his way, like me obeying laws, or going to work, or paying bills, or not killing anyone, the man always has to have his way because he's the man, well, fuck the man, fuck him up the ass until snot flies out of his nose, cause I'm sick of the man, and I'm sick of my job, and I'm sick of living at home with my senile grandparents, and I'm sick of following their rules after my parents died, and I'm sick of licking the smelly end of the plunger and pretending that it's a lollipop, I'm sick of the man always putting me in my place, so I'm gonna teach him a lesson right now by flying up into the air, but all of these people are in my way, jeez, can't they see I'm on a mission to beat the man, I have to beat the man, so I push some fatty fats out of my way so I can get closer to the stage and Eddie my love, Eddie, I am coming, please keep grooving to my pulsating ears with your exquisite fingers, I'm coming, I'm coming my love, out of my way you piece of shit, yeah, you want a piece of this, you want a piece of my naked flesh, yeah, I don't think so, my arms shove nimrods out of the way so I can get closer to Eddie, Eddie, I'm coming for you, together we can beat the man by wah-wahling on our pedal sticks, yes, Eddie, you can groove me just like you groove that guitar, but I'm not gay, no, I like women, I like women a lot, I just want you to, hey, out of my way, what, you think your yellow jacket is going to stop me, you think your big muscles are going to stop me, you think, hey, quit hitting me, OW, that hurts, ASSHOLE, you work for the man, don't you, you do, OW, QUIT HITTING ME, I'm on my knees down here, quit hitting me, that hurts, my hands cover my face from the pummeling blows, but my eyes see his vulnerable sausage, I'm really hungry and his sausage looks awfully good, yeah, so my jaw clamps onto his manhood, bites down, harder-harder-harder, make him beg and oh yeah-yeah-yeah-yeah, he's on his knees and I rise in victory, the man's henchman is screaming now, those screams don't sound like happy screams, no, they sound like screams of agony, oh, too bad, the man loses one of his co-workers, but I'm not done yet, no, I'm on an unstoppable mission, I have to shimmy up the rafter and jump so I can soar above the crowd and inspire them to rise up against the man and throw off their shackles, I have to inspire others to be free, and I can't believe how close I am to the top as my arms and legs zip up the metal girder, it feels so cool and smooth against my naked body, it feels like me and the pole are becoming one as I climb past one story and then another, and why does Eddie stop playing and why is the crowd booing and why are the fans, my fans, pelting me with trash, don't they know I'm doing this for them, don't they know I'm about to set them free from the empty void that the man has them in, don't they know I'm just like Jesus except without all that religious bullshit, don't they know that I'm doing this for them, well, I'm going to set them free anyway, my wings sprout and I'm going to soar away, I can see for miles and miles and miles and miles and miles, and I'm going to fly forever to let my people go, here I go, here I go, here I go, boo me all you want because I'm going to set you and me free, here I go, here I go, and I let go, I'M FREE I'M FREE I'M FREE and I'm flying-flying-flying-flying-flying right towards the ground, and I realize the split second before my body smashes face-first into the concrete and my spinal cord is pulverized that I never should have dropped acid.

The Earth is a Hollow Shell

Georg Koszulinski

1993

As a kid, I visited the ruins of the Koreshan utopian community in Estero, FL. What I remember about the site was a half-preserved set of buildings, an inverted globe of the world that revealed the continents on the inside, and I remember the glass windowpanes, thicker near the bottom after a hundred years of settling. One of the buildings looked like an old church. I don't remember many people being there. It's right there on the Estero River where I went camping once with grade school friends.

Just down the river, at its terminus in Estero Bay, was another site of an extinct community. The Calusa Indians lived here, built an island shell by shell, and were eventually wiped out by disease and forced labor brought on by the Spaniards. It was the Calusas who killed Ponce de Leon, piercing him with a spear as the conquistador came ashore. Ponce died eight days later in Cuba. All along the river you see the Calusa shell middens, and their manmade island rises maybe a hundred or more feet above sea level. Standing at the island's peak, one can see for hundreds of miles in every direction.

In 1896, the anthropologist Frank Hamilton Cushing spent five months digging through the south Florida muck unearthing a number of Calusa artifacts. The wooden masks and tools he found soon disintegrated once they came in contact with the air. Probably many a Florida subdivision were built over the bones of the ancient Calusa. One might speculate that this land in particular was cursed, dooming the Calusas and the Koreshans to extinction, but the history of colonization and genocide spans an entire continent, from *la Florida* to Alaska and everywhere in between.

1869-1993

Cyrus Teed has an illumination that convinces him he is the New Messiah. That same year he founds the Koreshan Unity. Teed believes in the hollow Earth theory: the globe is inhabited on its inner surface, and that the sun, moon, and astral bodies hang from the center. The universe is knowable, finite, and ordered.

In 1894, his followers arrive at the site in Estero. For sixty-seven years, they persist, and even thrive. They had a power generator at one point. Teed believed marriage was a form of legal slavery, but I speculate that he engaged in inappropriate sexual relations as many a cult leader tends to do (celibacy was the rule for the inner circle). In 1993, one hundred seventy-six acres of Koreshan land were sold to a development company. They built a gated community and golf course over the Koreshans' dead bodies.

The last Koreshan, Hedwig Michel, dies in 1982. What did Hedwig think of Ronald Reagan? Did she believe a utopian society was still possible? How could she retain a belief in something that every other human being in the world did not accept? I wish I could have met you, Hedwig.

2013

The parking lot is empty. The ranger tells me I've purchased the last copy of *Cellular Cosmogony*—Cyrus Teed's book of astral theories. I pass a sign that reads: "the tour starts here." The first building I come to is the one I remember most vividly. It's the theatre and art house where the inverted globe resides. "The universe is a hollow sphere." The stars were a hundred miles deep, what we saw were illusions: *what we saw were illusions.* It was said that Teed was trying to turn lead into gold; he was electrocuted, and had an illumination. Purchase the video for eighteen bucks.

I enter the gated community at the end of the road, where the ranger tells me the Koreshan cemetery is located, and drive down past the security checkpoint. I feel I'm being surveilled, and that I don't belong. I see people riding bicycles, playing golf in the distance— truly privileged people protected by the gates of their inverse prison. One of the stipulations of the land sale was that anyone who wanted to visit the Koreshan cemeteries be granted access, a kind of virus in their gated paradise that grants me entrance.

Past the golf courses and tennis courts, I find the cemetery hidden away in the pines. Down the trail, the graves are buried beneath the palmettos, grown over, dispersed here and there. I've come to pay my respects to the women and men of vision who dreamed of an alternative future. Cyrus Teed's ideas about a world without social and economic injustice never came to pass. The world is not a hollow sphere, and the gated community replaced the utopian one.

2079

Just like Hedwig, in the end I lost all my friends, living or dead. The connection to this landscape, or community or whatever you want to call it, is gone. For the eighteenth time in its geologic history, South Florida has gone underwater—an accelerated aftereffect of the anthropocene. One day, everything you love will die too. Perhaps the Earth is a hollow shell after all, and every beginning is an ending to a story you've never heard.

I've Come to Not Believe

Dah

*Where are you from
where are you going?*
Sometimes the absence of memory
is like spilled gasoline
that's impossible to retrieve

Trying to remember I tiptoe
like a child holding a secret
over my past
to somewhere near
not wanting to grow up

Time runs differently
when unsettled
light becomes piercing crescendos
wind feels like it's bleeding
emotional directions conflict

But none of it
belongs to this Lost Boy
running with imaginary friends
that I hide like whispers
but there are no *eternal youth* promises

My thoughts are ice-drops
freezing my flight
I clutch my heavy shadow
unwilling to conform
to worldly ways

In my heart Hope is a viper
when I breathe in
actuality strikes
then I exhale
the old man I've become

Those Who Stayed
Jennifer Pullen

I

W e remember the way the island looked after weeks and months
and years at sea. We remember the lush greenery, the sand as
white as linen and the sea as blue as the turquoise beads our wives
wore around their necks. We needed fresh water and so Odysseus
told us to land. The youngest of us, a lad of fourteen picked up along
the way, shook his head and refused to get off the ship. His limbs
were twigs breaking in the wind and he held his arms around his
knees to still the shaking. He said the island was a pit and he wouldn't
go near it. He was a stowaway from a strange port full of people who
drew on their faces with ink. Poor boy didn't realize what he'd stowed
away to. Privately, we thought him mad. We went to shore.

We dropped down into the shallows and the water lapped gently at
our knees, warm as milk straight from an udder. It was all we could
do not to drink it and roll in, wash the feeling of blood from our
bodies—the blood that wouldn't go away but none of us would ever
talk about or acknowledge feeling—because this water somehow felt
sanctified. We were all thinking about how we didn't want to embrace
our wives feeling filthy or try to get our children to remember us
while our nostrils still smelled like drying blood and our eyes still saw
the wolves and ravens circling the battlefield.

On the shore, we saw a group of people in beautiful flowing clothing
that the breeze made cling to bodies. The women were all soft curves,
full breasts, and rounded thighs. Then we realized that they were
all naked, the clothing was actually hair, draped like cloth and long
enough to touch the ground. They had dark hair which hung far past
their waists and twined like vines. One of us said they looked like
fertility goddesses or nymphs. We shushed him because we'd met one
spirit already and some of us had ended up as pigs.

Odysseus strode forward first, the warm weight of the water nothing
to him, and despite everything we couldn't help but worship him a
little. We thought it was good to be led by a magnificent man. He
bowed his red-gold head courteously but proudly to the assembled

people on the beach and asked for fresh water and provisions. He made the prospect of granting the request sound like a gift to the givers. Again, we admired him, our leader, and it seemed only natural that the women with their dark eyes and languid limbs would reach out to him, extending large white blossoms. As of yet we suspected nothing.

II

The island was all green glades and mossy rocks shaded by great trees. Bees and butterflies flew in dips and dives through the air and everywhere were little ponds brimming with floating flowers. The perfume sent up from the ponds made us dizzy and made everything seem benevolent and good. There were no buildings anywhere which should have helped us to understand that something was terribly wrong; but instead we watched, passive, as the people of the island wordlessly waded into the mirror-like ponds and scooped blossoms into their hands. They looked at those flowers like we remembered our wives looking at our children when they sucked at her breasts. As though they were looking at a beautiful inexplicable thing. But the constant rotting pain over families not seen for years and years was blessedly dull, distant, and somehow unimportant; we'd get home later so there was no need to worry about it just now.

The women pulled us down to the soft grassy banks and tilted the blossoms to our lips and poured nectar into our mouths until everything was sweetness. The nectar ran down our chests and those women licked off the nectar, eyes full of desire, and all we could think was it was so good to be touched so gently and savored so greatly. We warriors and sailors always talk about how much we long for women, but we do so crudely, making rude gestures while in our bunks and speaking rhapsodically about the glories of a woman's wet tight places. What we never talk about is that what we long for most is someone soft and warm and sweet to dilute our aloneness for an hour or two. We never talked of such things, but that is why we all let those women cover us in overflowing nectar, and later trail blossoms across our skin until we were dusted all over with pollen.

Once we drank the nectar the world seemed to glow and nothing in creation was as good as that soft grass and the buzzing of the bees as they landed on our skin. We watched the bees gather pollen on their fuzzy black and yellow bodies and then stumble as they tried to fly away. When they made it to the air their trajectory dipped downward and sideways in irregular swoops, and we remembered nights stumbling home heavy with wine. We slept.

Sometime in our sleep we felt rough hands shaking us, and for those of us who managed to open our eyes, we saw Odysseus leaning over us, shouting, and motioning wildly. But sleep was a siren and whatever our leader had to say could surely wait for another day.

III

Eventually we woke up and remembered our sleep-time visitor. We ran to the shore leaping over the still sleeping bodies of the island people, careless of being half dressed, or forgetting removed sword belts. But despite our rush when we got to the shore our ship was gone. We had no way of knowing how long we'd slept, hours or days. We had vague memories of brief moments of semi-wakefulness, of blossoms against our lips, of sucking pollen and nectar out of navels and cupping a woman's buttocks and sliding ourselves inside her. We examined our ribs and wrists and saw bones standing starker than usual. We'd lost days, maybe weeks, or even months in the lotus-blossom fog; our fellow men might even have made it home. We'd been left behind because we were too weak to resist the lotus-eaters. We were ashamed of that weakness. We made a pact to help each other resist the lotus flowers and alluring nectar. We were determined to find a way off the island.

We tried to find something to eat other than the lotus nectar. But the island, so fertile and verdant looking, had no birds and no squirrels, nothing small and easy to kill, nor anything large or dangerous. The trees had no fruit. We ate grass instead, and tried not to watch the islanders as they drank the nectar and ate the blossoms. We didn't understand how they could be so plump despite eating nothing but the lotus. We were so hungry. We found a little stream trickling over rocks at the center of the island, but there were no fish in it to tickle into our palms. But we stuck our faces straight into its clear cool shallows, and drank. We were afraid to go near the ponds, for the scent of the nectar had a gravity to it, a pull that we could feel even from a distance.

The islanders mostly ignored us. Apparently, we'd lost our novelty and therefore our interest. It hurt our pride a bit, to find out those willing women liked the lotus flowers better than us. But our hunger took care of desires like that anyway.

Eventually we found some shellfish and little crabs in the shallows by the sea, and cracked open the shells to slurp out the cool salty flesh. But we were still hungry. Sometimes we'd catch one of our number standing very still, staring towards one of the ponds, eyes full of craving. We'd move him away, gently, because it was part of our pact never to admit that we felt the same pull.

Once the lotus nectar wore off, we remembered our families. Some of us cried over abandoned wives and sons who wouldn't have anyone to teach them how to sail or hunt. Some of us gathered pretty pebbles off the shore, said we'd give them to our daughters to play with some day, and that each pebble was a story. Others of us suffered in silence and tried not to think of fresh bread, and our mothers and fathers growing older and greyer, of wives getting re-married, of someone else sleeping in our bed.

We grew desperate, pulled branches off trees and made vines into ropes. We didn't have axes so we lashed together fallen logs and tried to make a raft. We spent days dragging the raft toward the shore, our underfed bodies too weak to move it quickly. We put it in the water, all climbed aboard, some of us hanging off the edge, and kicking to propel it through the tide. We barely got far enough to lose sight of the trees by the shore before we noticed that the vines were disintegrating in the water. We had to turn back or drown.

We took off most of our clothes and braided them together to make ropes. This time we got so far that the island became a little dot in the distance. We felt triumphant, hopeful. We had bags made from leaves full of water and carefully hoarded and dried shellfish. Surely, we'd find another island before we all died.

Then we saw the sharks. Vast hordes of fins swimming back and forth. We tried to go around the sharks, we circled the island, but everywhere the fins cut the water. Some of us muttered about curses, others made the sign against evil, while a few privately decided that the Fates had made up their minds, and there was no use struggling against those Weavers. Again, we had to turn back.

IV

Our pact was broken, our unity shattered. What was the use of striving if no success was possible? We wandered the island aimlessly, just for something to do, anything to relieve the boredom, to not stare at each other, to not let each other see the darkness pooling in our eyes. Inland, we found a dried-up pond, and around it skeletons, laying in an attitude of sleep, white as the lotus blossoms under the sun. Staring at those skeletons, eye sockets wide, finger bones splayed, we realized suddenly that the pond had dried up but the lotus eaters couldn't be bothered to move, to find another source of water and blossoms, and they probably simply laid by the pond until they died.

When we woke and saw one or two of us missing, we weren't surprised. A few of us drowned ourselves. A few of us walked past a pond surrounded by lotus eaters, saw a woman open her gown of hair and spread her pale thighs while proffering a blossom in her hands, and went to her. A few of us stopped eating and watched our flesh dwindle with satisfaction. A few of us still eat the shellfish and pull up grass and choke it down, never out of sight of the sea, watching the waves for a sail. The best spot to watch is the cliffs on the north side of the island, high, far away from ponds and soft grass, a rocky place scoured by wind. There, if a ship comes near, they can't possibly be missed, and we can wave a flag made from one of our tattered white tunics, and pray that they see us. We'll warn them and then hop aboard. We don't keep track of days, so we don't have to count how long we've been waiting, how long we've been watching, or how long the wind has blown drafts of pollen so near.

My Fifth Sense

Teresa H. Janssen

I pulled in my breath a whiff at a time. Sourness came from the skin, the hair, and the lips of the contractor installing our kitchen cabinets.

"I think he's ill," I told my husband.

"How can you tell?" he said.

It was his smell. Three weeks later, we read the man's obituary.

I have a good nose, even for the raw and unpleasant. Some "bad" smells are my favorites because of the memories they bring. I remember the stink of the latrine behind the best hiding place at summer camp, my father's beer-laced breath as he hugged me, the fumes from the gas pump my sixteenth summer as I filled the tank of my mom's '69 Bonneville, the acrid trace of manure from the ponies that lived in our barn, my Lab's pungent farts in the last months of his life, and the sweat of men I have loved.

At night, I sleep with my window open. I want to smell the rain on pavement and grass, the morning sun on dewy juniper, the lilacs below my room, and the scent of snow in the clouds. If the light is too bright, I wear eyeshades; the world too loud, I put in earplugs. I sleep on my back, my nose in the air.

I appreciate my sense of smell day and night because I fear I may someday lose it. *Anosmia*, the loss of the sense of smell, like a canary in a coal-mine, can be an indicator of a more serious disease.

I'm a downwinder. I was born in Richland in south-central Washington State during the atomic era. The Hanford Nuclear Production Complex, six miles from Richland, was established in 1943 as part of the Manhattan Project. Hanford was the site of the B-Reactor, the world's first full-scale plutonium production reactor designed by Enrico Fermi and built by DuPont. By the time I was born in 1958, there were eight reactors in operation and five centers that processed plutonium for our nuclear bombs and warheads. Hanford was at its peak production between 1956 and 1965, when my family lived there. During its first twenty-eight years of operation, significant amounts of radioactive materials, including Iodine-131, were released into the Columbia River, into the soil, and into the air. Radioactive particles drifted down river to the Pacific and downwind toward Richland and the eastern part of the state, into Oregon, Idaho, and Montana. We, who consumed the water, food, and milk produced in the area, ingested these radio-nuclides.

Hanford Health Information Network, in collaboration with the Washington State Department of Health, finally publicized data in the 1980's about the health effects of Hanford's operations. The reports determined that residents who lived downwind from Hanford or who used the Columbia River downstream were exposed to elevated doses of radiation that placed them at increased risk for various cancers and other diseases. High doses of Iodine-131 have been positively linked to thyroid cancer.

The National Research Foundation and EPA have verified that women are much more susceptible to radiation-induced cancers because of radio-sensitive organs: the breasts, ovaries, and thyroid. The 2006 National Research Council's BEIR VII report found that women with an equal level of radiation exposure are 52 percent more likely than men to develop cancer while an EPA report puts the estimate of likelihood as high as 58 percent.

I started thinking about this when I was in my mid-twenties. I was living in Florida for the first time, teaching international students, and had become enamored with the smells of night-blooming jasmine, orange blossom, the bark of live oak, and the earthy decay of swamplands. That was the year I became dog-tired, developed a chronic sore throat, lost my sense of smell, and then my appetite. I was diagnosed with autoimmune thyroiditis. That meant my thyroid was no longer doing its job producing the hormones I needed for a healthy metabolism. Thyroiditis is associated with an increased risk for thyroid cancer.

A specialist recommended I do whatever I could to reduce the stress in my life before going onto a thyroid supplement. My job as a young post-grad teaching all-male university classes *was* stressful. I had just gotten married—the wedding a happy event, but anxiety-inducing. Driving home from work in my oven-hot Ford Maverick was taxing my body. So I quit my job and moved far away—out of the country. My symptoms went away. I could smell again. My appetite returned and my energy, too. The specialist told me to be watchful: my thyroid might wreak havoc later in my life. I had bought some time.

Being vigilant, for me, means watching for one of the signs of thyroid disease—the loss of smell. A 2014 research study at the University of Chicago concluded that the onset of anosmia can be a precursor of declining health. It found that those subjects who were unable to detect odors were several times more likely to die within the next five years than those who could smell. Since the olfactory nerve, which dangles into our nostrils, is the only nerve exposed to open air, damage to its receptors can be a warning sign of exposure to toxins. Loss of the sense of smell is a possible predictor of morbidity because the tip of the olfactory nerve is continuously regenerated with stem cells. Declining smell can be an indicator of the body's inability to repair itself.

I have come to cherish my sense of smell. Sometimes called the Fifth Sense, smell is one of those things that we hardly appreciate until it is gone. Anosmia can result from a virus or flu, exposure to medications or chemicals, cancer, a traumatic brain injury, or chronic disease, such as diabetes, multiple sclerosis, and Parkinson's. Processed in the same part of the brain as memory, the sense of smell is closely tied to emotion and long-term recollection. Its loss can be a precursor of dementia or Alzheimer's. Most nasal events cause only a temporary loss of smell, but for twenty percent of those affected, anosmia is permanent.

Its effects can be devastating. Much of our pleasure around food is due to aroma since most flavors are experienced through a combination of odor and taste. Its loss can result in a disinterest in eating, weight loss, and melancholy. To no longer be able to smell fresh bread, a ripe strawberry, buttered popcorn, the salty sea air, the scent of one's child or spouse, or discern the moods of others can cause a feeling of isolation and detachment from the world. It can be dangerous to be unable to smell rotten food, smoke, gas or chemical leaks.

Professor Barry C Smith, co-director and founder of the Centre for the Study of the Senses, says, "Studies have shown that people who lose their sense of smell end up more severely depressed and for longer periods of time than people who go blind. No place or person smells familiar anymore. Losing that emotional quality to your life is incredibly hard to deal with."

Our sense of smell is primal. We think we choose our partners based on looks, personality, or background. But studies have shown that pheromones—those subliminal airborne, chemical signals that exude from our skin and hair, the strongest of which come from our armpits—play a major role in sexual attraction. This is thought to be due to pheromone sensors, the pea-size vomeronasal organ in the tissue of the nasal septum, or a newly discovered pair of pheromone nerves that run from the nose directly to the brain.

Every human has a unique "odor print" like a fingerprint called MHC. Parents with widely differing MHC produce offspring with stronger immune systems. For the good of the species, we are attracted to those with a less familiar odor print. When my children ask me for dating advice, I usually tell them to follow their instincts, but perhaps I should tell them to trust their noses.

Smell has been essential to the survival of humans. In utero, the infant smells and tastes the amniotic fluid that resembles the smell of his mother's breast milk. A newborn placed on his mother's tummy will wiggle towards the breast for nursing and, by the end of the first week, can distinguish his mother's milk from that of another woman. When a mom and baby snuggle, bathing in each other's scents, oxytocin, the "feel good" hormone, is released by both, key to mother-baby bonding.

In those early weeks after the birth of my first child, exhausted from nights of sporadic sleep, insecure about my ability to care for this helpless, hairless human, afraid to leave her alone, even to shower, and pungent from spending half the day in my nightgown infused with spilled milk, spit-up, and the pong of post birth, I was relieved to know that my baby daughter preferred my aroma to that of anyone else. No matter the intensity of my body odor, she thought I smelled like a rose.

Richland, nicknamed Atomic City, was planned by the Army Corps of Engineers and built and operated by the government for workers at the nuclear complex and related service industries. My father took a job there setting up new drugstores. My family found housing in a government-owned duplex for a token rent. Many of their needs were provided for, from free transit to light bulbs. Every other evening for half the year, a truck would lumber through their neighborhood spraying DDT to kill the mosquitoes. My parents would call my siblings in from play, wait for the sprayer to pass, then send them back out into the strangely sweet evening air.

I imagine, after my parents' chaotic childhoods during World War II, the exceptional order of the place was reassuring. My parents moved there to save money for a down payment to buy their first home. The job in Richland paid more than my father could earn west of the Cascades where he and my mom had grown up. They had no idea that taking the new job would expose their children to a barrage of toxic chemicals. They knew little about DDT. They had probably never heard of Iodine-131.

A 2002 U.S. Department of Health and Human Services report summarized I-131 exposure research findings for health practitioners. It confirmed that during pregnancy, the mother's thyroid has an increased rate of I-131 uptake. Since I-131 crosses into the placenta, the fetal thyroid takes up and stores iodine in increasing amounts. During the first postpartum week, the infant's thyroid activity increases up to fourfold before stabilizing. Because children's thyroids are so small, they are at a higher risk from radioiodine. About one-quarter of the iodine taken in by the mother is secreted in breast milk, which adds an additional risk factor for a breastfed infant.

The BEIR VII report discussed increased risks if a woman is exposed to significant doses of nuclear-related radiation in early pregnancy when organs are being formed. Fetal malformations can occur when a woman receives a radiation dose between the 10th and 40th day of pregnancy high enough to cause mutations, but not high enough to abort the fetus. It expressed concern that the effects of radiation on fetal formation are a particularly serious health issue for female infants whose ovaries are formed while they are still in utero. Mutational effects of radiation can cause multigenerational health issues and may increase a daughter's risks for infertility, reproductive problems, and ovarian cancer.

In a 2015 report, Dr. Barbara Cohn, researcher at the Public Health Institute of Berkeley, CA, concluded that women who had a high exposure to DDT while in their mother's womb had almost four times the risk of developing breast cancer by age 52.

I was conceived, born, and breastfed for six-months in Richland. My in-utero exposure to both I-131 and DDT makes me more than a little bit wary about my health. I have my thyroid checked regularly.

In my twenties, I wondered whether I would ever be able to have children. I wondered whether my uterus had been somehow mutated in the womb by radiation exposure. I worried that when pregnant, my thyroid would again go on strike, predisposing me to miscarriage. That's why the birth of my first healthy child was so incredible and why the miscarriage of my second was so devastating. Women who lose a baby often fear they will never again be able to support a full-term pregnancy. I was fortunate. Following my miscarriage, I bore three more healthy children.

When I was still a baby, my parents moved away from Richland and bought a house near Puget Sound where my father found work in another drugstore. A few years later on April 29th, we were hit by a 6.5 magnitude earthquake. It caused chimneys, factory stacks, and sidewalks to collapse, and a crack in the dome of the state capitol.

I still live in earthquake country, just miles from where the San Juan Plate is being subducted beneath the North American Plate. We, who live in this place of high seismic risk, know that a great megathrust earthquake, "the really big one," is overdue. We are reminded every few years with tremors; the last significant one sixteen years ago when a 6.8 magnitude quake caused over $2 billion in damage. Brick fascia and cornices fell from buildings, a buttress splintered beneath the capitol building, and new fissures appeared on its dome.

I think of cancer and earthquakes the same way. Sometimes they give us warnings, but usually they arrive with no notice at all. They can strike at any time. They can be scary. They can cause cracks in our foundations. They can force us to make big changes in our lives and figure out what is most important. They make us appreciate what we've got. They can be fatal. I won't be surprised if one of them hits during my life. I am aware of my risks.

I panicked a few weeks ago when I had a mean virus. For days, I couldn't smell a thing. I feared my sense of smell might never return and my health would go with it. I thought my fate had caught up with me. Then, one evening, I smelled the cod in the microwave. Hallelujah! I never thought I would rejoice at the odor of day-old reheated fish.

Our sense of smell is most acute between the ages of thirty and sixty. After sixty-five, the average person may lose twenty-five percent of the ability to identify odors. With practice; however, as any perfumer, sommelier, or coffee aficionado can tell you, we can enhance our sense of smell. By consciously linking smell and experience, we can increase our olfactory intelligence and enhance our scent memories.

My babies smelled of new skin and breast milk, like sugar in chamomile tea. When they were school-age and finally in bed, I would stand at the washer and bury my nose in grass-stained trousers, chocolate-tainted shirts, and sheets that smelled of sleep— exhausted, yet already nostalgic for innocence lost.

When they were teenagers, I sniffed their hair to know where they'd been.

"Stop smoking," I told my son.

"How did you know?" he said.

I twitched my nose, but he didn't notice. "I have my ways."

My husband smells mildly soapy like the William's shaving cake he lathers in a mug and spreads across his cheeks with a soft brush. When he puts pizza in the oven then leaves the house to chop wood, I can smell the crust burning even if I'm upstairs and run to save it. Then I call him in, and he thanks me, and as we crunch the darkened ends, the piquant aroma of yeast, garlic, and basil mixes with the tang of sap and fresh cedar and the musk of autumn leaves. I can hardly swallow for joy.

Photographic Evidence

Robert Hoffman

There is no way, of course, to enter
a photograph, to touch the light of years

gone by, inspired, infused, by a moment
of collected elements; of photons,

electrons, paper, film, and aperture
gap; the exposure of light, the negative

touch of emotional prey. Though the sound
is lost, it can very well be heard

between the emulsion and light waves,
the surface shine, the image just below,

where black and white and color is the sound of
shuffling, the sound of cheese before the snap,

the sound of tension below Aunt Claudia's
grinding molars and tendon cheeks, along the jaw.

Her pursed lips and brow-scowl can't hide
the anger behind high gloss and film in front

of the sanitarium a hundred
years ago, the sigh between the taker

and the taken, who is trapped, the presence
of eons of routine evolution.

Stray
Anara Guard

John says not to feed it and, of course, I won't, but it's difficult to listen to the sound of a cat yowling and do nothing. When we open the back door, it runs off; but, soon enough, comes right back again. It's a tabby with gray and black stripes. No collar. Not too thin or scraggly. I do wish it would stop meowing. John runs the garbage disposal and the racket seems to drive the cat away. I wonder where it lives.

Today, the cat leapt onto my kitchen windowsill and sat there, staring in at me while I washed the dishes. I thought perhaps it was thirsty, so I poured water into a saucer and brought it out onto the porch. By the time I opened the door, balancing the saucer in my other hand so that it wouldn't spill all over the threshold, the cat was gone. I left the water on the porch and later, the dish was bone dry. I think I'll keep leaving water outside. John can't object to making sure that a poor creature isn't thirsty. It doesn't cost him anything.

The water disappears from time-to-time but not every day. Occasionally, a dead beetle floats upside down on the surface. Don't drink if you can't swim, my dad used to say. It was a funny line until a car full of drunk teenagers veered off the causeway one night. They weren't found for six days. I saw a picture of their car being hauled up by a crane. Water poured from the open windows like rivulets of tears and you just knew that four bodies were inside, rotting away. I hate to even think of it.

The cat is back, pacing the windowsill, and yowling. I wonder if it's in heat. John says, "Do tomcats holler when they're in heat?" How do you know it's a tom? He says he looked, of course, and then I feel foolish. So now I know it's a *he*. Do you think he's calling for a female to recognize his need?

I ask our neighbors whether they're missing a gray-striped cat. The woman next door whose name I don't know doesn't bother to unlatch her screen door to talk to me. Behind the grid of the screen her face is dark and remote. Her husband is allergic so, no, they don't have any pets.

On the other side are the Chalmers. It has been a while since I'd seen either one of them. I knock loudly and wait because I know it can take them a long time to hobble to the door. They're so deaf, I doubt they've heard the cat wailing away.

"No, dear." Mrs. Chalmers leans on her walker. Blue veins marble her thin hands. "Isn't it yours? We saw the little bowl you put out. We thought you adopted it."

I think that's funny but John doesn't see the humor. "See, you're just encouraging it to come back."

The cat no longer flees when I open the back door. He sits and watches me. His fine head bears the shape of the letter M formed by black hairs in amongst the gray. I try out different names on him: Max, Mickey, Maurice. He blinks in response, but none of them are right.

It's raining hard. Our bedroom window rattles in the wind and keeps me awake. I wonder where the cat is: indoors somewhere and dry or huddled beneath a tree, soaked and cold? I get up when I think I hear his scratch at the back door. But when I unlock and peek out, it's nothing but blowing rain. Just after breakfast, the sun comes out and there he is, not the least bit damp. So, he must have some other place to go. I've decided his name is Mystery.

I think Mystery howls because he's hungry. I buy a little packet of kitty treats and sprinkle a few next to his water dish. He sniffs at them as if he isn't sure whether to eat them or not. Then he laps them up, one at a time. His tongue is remarkably pink.

Mystery doesn't show up until right after John leaves for work; I don't know how. I check the back porch as John leaves by the front door: empty. Then I run to the front of the house and watch him turn right at the end of the walk. I trot back to the kitchen. The cat hasn't arrived yet. I lope to the living room and press my face against the window: there goes John, just turning the corner to the bus stop. To the kitchen again, breathless and full of hope. Mystery sits on my windowsill, as calm and still as if he has been there for hours.

Does he hear the front door close or can he recognize John's figure as he walks to the bus stop? John has a funny way of bouncing on the balls of his feet with each stride. I would never mention it to him, but it does make him look a bit silly, like he's seen too many Monty Python routines. He used to watch the show and he enjoyed the dead parrot, the bureaucrats gone amok. Now that he dresses in a coat and tie every day and rides the bus to his job in the Financial District, it's not so amusing, I guess.

"Have you been feeding that stray?" John holds the package of treats, nearly empty now. There's no point in responding; the answer is obvious. "You know you're just encouraging it to hang around." He rattles the package at me. It sounds ominous, that nearly hollow noise.

Sometimes I think that John doesn't even like me anymore. Four years of marriage, but it feels longer. He has a certain way of looking at me while we sit at the table over dinner, like he can't remember why he ever sought out my company. As if we're on a blind date and he's already thinking what he'll say to the friend who set him up: thanks, but no thanks, pal.

We undress beside our opposite sides of the bed, facing away from each other, strangers. Yet in the morning, our bodies are curled together, warm and close, as if all the slights and barbs evaporated during sleep.

I find myself in the pet food aisle at the supermarket. So many choices! Different formulas for kittens and older cats, indoor or outdoor, special diets for weight control and for hairballs. Mystery seems in between kitten and old, so I ignore those varieties and concentrate on figuring out whether he'll prefer chicken, salmon, beef, or lamb. I sniff at the bags and settle on beef flavor with grains and greens added, although I can't imagine why a cat would care about greens.

The bag is small enough to fit in the bottom cupboard behind my juicer, which I haven't used in a long time. I feel like a kid hiding a chocolate bar in the back of my sock drawer. I'm not afraid of John's reaction, but I like to avoid confrontation. I don't want to see him scowl.

It's not like I place his food out every day at the same time. I remember my college psych class and all those readings on Skinnerian reinforcement. Give treats at random times for greater responsiveness, shaping in the right direction. When Mystery is quiet, I reward him and he allows me to stroke his head, just above the M. His fur is silky soft. I scratch beneath his ears and he rubs against my hand, purring his pleasure.

It's a funny thing with secrets. You might think that you make your choice once: keep the secret or not, lie or tell the truth. But really, it's more like watching a mouse hole; you have to pay attention to every movement and decide whether this is the moment to respond, over and over. Every day, after I fill Mystery's bowl, I have to choose whether to slip the bag back into its hiding place or leave it where anyone could see it. So far, each day, the crumpled bag is returned to its dark cupboard. Little lies repeated daily, becoming more efficient and adept with practice. But not easier. It feels like a cavity slowly growing larger, the black spot that gets bigger, more painful, harder to ignore.

How happy Mystery has become. His fur is glossier than ever. When he snakes around my bare legs, it feels like someone is trailing a silk scarf against my calves. He rarely yowls now. He leaps to the windowsill in a single, athletic bound, and waits quietly for me. I've taken to leaving the back-door open while I fill his bowl but he never crosses the threshold. After he eats, we have a bit of a cuddle. Sometimes he'll nap in a sunny spot on the porch or in the yard, but not when John is home. Never when John is home.

I have a routine now, but not my own. It is Mystery who determines when I get up, when I reach the kitchen, how quickly I reach for his dish. It's his decision whether I return to my desk to work, or remain on the porch for head scratching and a thorough going-over with the soft-bristled brush. He is my first task of the morning and my last of the night.

Mrs. Chalmers totters out her back door while Mystery and I are just finishing our morning routine.

"What a nice cat you have," she says in her deaf, quavering voice.

"Oh, he's not my—" I start to say, but then stop myself. Is he mine? He doesn't seem to belong to anyone else.

"Thank you," I say. I'm not sure she hears me. She laboriously shakes out a dishcloth, showering bread crumbs into the grass. For the birds, I guess. Mystery will like that.

Later, I worry what might happen if she mentions my cat to John.

I can't sleep. Cats are nocturnal, but where do they go? I slip out of bed and into my sweats. Outside, the night air is cool and very still. A train rumbles in the distance but the usual traffic sounds have all died away. I creep into the yard in search of Mystery. It's an odd sensation to slink about as if I were a burglar, watching the shadows for movement, looking for his green eyes gleaming in the dark. He's not here.

But if I were a cat, I'd run from this strange figure in a sweatshirt. I'm too clumsy and loud, too visible under the streetlight's glare. Best to stand quietly in the shadows, let my eyes adjust to this black and white world before I learn to walk with padded foot. I hover in a shaded corner, breathe shallowly, study which way the breeze blows. And after a time, a skinny yellow cat prowls down the alley. It sniffs the air until it catches my scent. Its eyes flicker over me. Then, satisfied I am neither foe nor threat, it continues on its way. Before dawn, I tiptoe back to bed.

If you nap twice during the day, you can have many waking hours to explore after dark. I've learned there are raccoons in the city; they scuttle around the trash bins and dumpsters, searching for a way to pry the lids open. And those little mounds of dirt on people's lawns are made by skunks as they dig for grubs. I can recognize their white stripes from down the block now, often before I catch their odor on the wind.

The night holds its own rhythms and cycles. Time is marked by the hissing of sprinklers and by the newspaper route, the latest edition thudding against the walk like the slow ticking of a grandfather clock. I take pride in never letting the delivery driver pick me up in his headlights. I dress in navy, gray, dark green. For shadows are not merely black—they contain charcoal, iron, smoke, and ash. And as I walk, Mystery flows with me. He finds me, even blocks from home. Without making a sound he appears, and we patrol our city together. He walks close by my shin, guiding me as if I am blind.

John says, "I'm worried about you. I call home and you don't answer." I tell him I was asleep, but his anxious look doesn't ease. "Every day? Are you sick?" No, no. Just tired. I think he wakes up now and lies there until I return. There are smudges beneath his eyes and once, just as I reached the alley, I thought I heard our back-door open. I crouched in the inky shade as he searched the yard for me but his eyes weren't accustomed to our ways. After a few minutes, the door closed with a sigh and I was free to go.

John insists that I see a doctor. Too many times he had found me napping when he came home, with no dinner ready and my hair snarled like a crazy person's thoughts. "It's not normal to sleep so much," he says. At last I agree, and he takes the day off work to drive me to the clinic. At the curb, he pulls over and lets me out, watches me rotate through the revolving door and into the lobby. I look over my shoulder and he's still there, engine idling, craning his head to make sure I step into the elevator. So I do.

What a waste of time, these sleepy hours of sagging in a hard, plastic chair as I wait to be seen, to have blood drawn, to learn what was observed beneath the microscope. Nothing is found in my blood or my throat, no sign of anemia, infection, thrush. I've lost weight from all my walking, but the doctor can find no cause for my daytime naps and I don't tell him that I'm becoming a nocturnal animal.

When John picks me up, he is strangely lighthearted. His fingers drum the steering wheel to a jaunty tune that I can't hear. He takes me out for dinner and I ask for tuna, steak tartare, and a glass of milk. He blinks but pretends not to notice.

I can't find Mystery! It's been two nights and he hasn't shown up for our rendezvous. People fear going out at night as if the city is full of murderers, but the real dangers are fast cars, rat poison, and vicious dogs. I lope through the alleys, afraid that I'll stumble across his lifeless body. I call for him beneath windows and down breezeways, between fence boards and under parked trucks, but all my voice does is disturb the air.

At daylight, I drag myself home as the city comes alive. It is too much color, too much noise. Who can tolerate such turmoil?

John waits in the kitchen. "It's no use searching," he says. "The cat is gone." He looks at me with an unswerving gaze. "I caught it in a live trap. And took it away."

If you hurt him ... My hands curl into fists; my teeth are ready.

"Of course, I didn't hurt it. I took it to a shelter. They'll find a good home."

No! I am his home. But John won't give me the address, no matter how loudly I wail.

I paw through the phone book. There are six shelters listed and I call them all. Two say that they had a gray-striped tomcat but no longer: one was given away; the other put down. I snarl at the phone, spit at John. My heart howls in pain.

That man thinks he has removed the temptation by trapping my Mystery, and now perhaps I'll stay put, no longer stray at night. But he's much too late. The light gets shorter every day as autumn stretches past the equinox. The dark descends toward me, I have been waiting for it, the night belongs to me, and I move through it without making a sound.

Lena
Toti O'Brien

A fterwards, her husband comes close.
At this point, I'm taking things down. Literally on the floor, fitting my accordion into its case. I look up. He asks me if I'd mind meeting his wife at their table. I accept the invitation with grace. Gratitude, in fact—chance encounters with the audience are the highlights of my performing career.

Lena is pretty. Her hair, cut in an usually unflattering fashion, looks quite gorgeous around her miniature face. Well preserved, her beauty needs no makeup. The only hint at age (illness perhaps) is the deep halo encircling her large cobalt eyes.

Such color … not too light, as in those irises which make you feel lost, sucking you into a quasi-vertigo. Not so dense, so thick, to make you bounce against a cold metal shield. Hers is the ideal blue—or the opposite, the most natural one. A sea at sunset, where you can trustfully dive, feeling both safe and free. Where you can dive stark naked, as I do, sinking with no hesitation, simultaneously taking her hand.

She holds mine firmly, and I know the feeling. I've done this before—put my hand in that of an old or sick person. One who can't move, do things, go places … one who stays and remembers. When they take your hand, something comes through. It is startling—a current, a tide.

What's in it? Lots of past, of course—concentrated and distilled, vibratile, and warm. And a hook pulling future in. Not their future—they have none and they know it. But they thread in, nail down, anchor between their palm and yours any future, all future. Grab it if you like. If you want some for yourself or could pass some down. Like they're doing right now, letting it through your skin … this transfusion, this spark of hope.

Lena doesn't let go of me with her hand or her eyes. Not even when she acknowledges her husband's conversation. Warmly, kindly, she pays attention to his words, but she doesn't drop me. I've been singing songs of the land she left eight decades ago. She has enjoyed them. She still speaks the language and she proves it, encouraged by her spouse.

He seems eager to please her, more eager to push her into a youthful state of mind. As if such immersion could operate a reversal in time, subtract a few minutes to the clock, postpone something. In fact, she is pleasing him, slipping in and out of the magic cloak he forces on her. She goes back into the immigrant girl's skin—re-living those moments—then returns to her mature self, to the culture that's now her own.

Does she care? It doesn't look like it. She doesn't depend on memories, doesn't long for lost something. No. She's got it all here, cupped in her palm. Alive. Breathing. But he's nervous, uneasy, as if he feared, suspected, knew something she doesn't know.

We of course mention her striking eyes, not so uncommon in her native South: a residue of Viking domination. They have searched her genes, tracking her back to Finnish roots. Not unheard of. Still, when she appeared in the midst of her chestnut brothers and sisters, the villagers couldn't help gossiping. The husband likes this bit of local lore he relates with gusto. Where did she come from? Apparently out of the blue, the sky, distant seas … an angel. With these eyes he fell in love and still is.

He recalls the story of her father, who came to California through Canada. A long journey down the coast. Years of labor before he could send for the family. Wife, small children, and the teen girl—Lena. "Those were brave people," he says proudly, though he is not one of them. But he has married one.

Brave. She stares at me quietly. Without words, she lets it all come through: the intrepid father, the hard work, the long journey West, North, then South, along the endless coast. Oceans, oceans, oceans. Things dear left behind. Things strange to take in. Bridges to build then to cross unblinkingly, holding always, holding steadily.

To life—this round, simple thing. Hold it. Then let it go.

Shuttered Box
Lana Bella

Sounds echoed out of years.
The girl walked down a hallway
to find time entangled in ropes,
sins poured out from jars of dust,
holy psalms fed to lips without
weight.

Knees brittle where she turned to
leave, bones cut holes into shadow,
feeling to the way instincts grew
crops from this shuttered box.
Smoke in her memory, she stood
touched by the abstinence of life,
all done up in ever-shifting plain
of ghosts.

Here, snug in night's curvature,
lantern swinging in hand, her feet
grew to the valleys of floorboard,
pearl-adorned shoes stepped over
the bones of a forgotten century.

Not a Cry You Hear at Night
William Cass

Will stayed at the bed and breakfast on a lark. He worked from home in software development and only drove down to the company headquarters north of San Diego overnight for meetings once a month or so. When he did, he always stayed in a regular motel close enough to walk to the headquarters. But, he happened upon the bed and breakfast one day while surfing on the internet. It was a weathered, shingled collection of rooms, each with a themed décor that sat on a bluff over the ocean in one of the little coastal towns along old Highway 101. It wasn't very far from the headquarters, so he thought: what the hell. That it was the kind of place his ex-wife would have sought out didn't enter his mind at the time.

His meeting that afternoon included an early dinner, so he didn't check in until after eight. It was a Thursday, late fall, and the place seemed practically empty. His room was in a corner on the second floor and had a peek-a-boo view of the ocean from its bay window. Its theme was "Country Pine." All the furniture and molding was of that variety, the wallpaper and bedspread shared a similar rural print, and there were different sorts of wooden ducks everywhere: ducks on the shelves, on top of the armoire, in the bathroom, even the identical bedside lamps had ducks built into their pine bases. He laughed a little looking around the room, then unpacked the bottle of Merlot from his bag and poured himself a glass.

He took off his shoes, stretched out on the bed, sipped, and watched the distant white froth of waves through the window as they approached the shore. It was then that he thought of his ex-wife. She'd left a year and a half before with a fellow teacher right after the school year ended. They moved immediately to Northern California and found teaching jobs. It had been a complete surprise to Will; she'd never given any indication of discontent and he'd suspected nothing. Over time, he guessed he thought about it a little less. He tried to convince himself that was the case. But, he thought about her lying there. She'd found a similar place for them to stay up on the Oregon coast during their honeymoon a decade earlier just after their college graduation.

He noticed the guest journal when he poured his second glass of wine. It was on the bedside table next to where he'd set the bottle. He opened it and began reading entries from people who had stayed in the room over the years. Most of them had to do with the hospitality, the beauty of the setting, the quaintness of the town, the delicious breakfasts, the relief and relaxation of the visit, the unique décor. A number commented on the ducks, some with bemusement and humor; several differed on the total tally of ducks in the room.

Will worked his way slowly through the journal until he came to the last entry. He frowned when he first read it and sat up straight. He read it again, then lowered the journal onto his lap, and shook his head. The entry read:

I've snuck away to write this and I'm sorry to ruin the rosy tone of these entries. I hope they continue and I hope to write one myself someday when I'm finally freed from this hell of a relationship I'm in. When I'm finally out from under his controlling grip. Why do I always end up with men who can think with only their cocks? He makes me do things I hate and I despise myself for them. I know that I have a better spirit inside and that whoever can help save me from him will see that. Until then, I'll just hope and pray.

It was signed with the name, Tessa, scribbled so hard that its image was pressed into the following page. A shattered heart that she'd drawn across the entry made it difficult to decipher some of the words. It was dated two days earlier. Will closed the journal, turned off the lamp, and sat back in the darkness thinking and listening to the quiet tumble and retreat of the waves.

He didn't sleep well and rose early. He went for a jog on the beach in the fog. By the time he'd returned to the room, showered, and dressed, the fog had begun to lift and a little sunlight sifted through the window's blinds. He sat on the edge of the bed and reached for his shoes underneath. His hand felt a folded piece of paper there; he brought it out and unfolded the paper. It was a computer printout of directions to the bed and breakfast. A shattered heart identical to the one in the journal was drawn over the center of the page. He followed the directions backwards. They led to an address in a Los Angeles suburb not far from his own. He sat blinking for a moment before folding the paper into his pocket and putting on his shoes.

After breakfast, Will packed, drove to the headquarters for another meeting, and then was headed back home on the freeway by ten o'clock. He stopped for gas just south of his normal exit and consulted the folded paper again. He had nothing special to do and nowhere he had to be; his work was done for the week. So, he drove past his exit and followed the directions on the paper the short distance to where they began.

He parked under a tree across the street from the address, which was a small, drab bungalow in an older neighborhood that bordered an industrial park. An empty birdbath stood next to a pepper tree in the front yard of patchy, dry grass. A corner of the screen on the outer front door was torn and moved slightly in the breeze. The front door was open, but the inside of the house was dark behind it. A newspaper in its plastic wrap sat on the front step. The paint on the black sedan in the driveway was faded, but the vanity plate on the rear bumper looked new; it read: TESSA1. It was still, quiet. There was no traffic.

About five minutes passed before the screen door opened and a woman about his age came out onto the front step. She wore a flowered cotton robe, loosely tied around her thin waist. Her shoulder-length hair was brown and, although unkempt, Will inhaled at her hardened beauty. When she bent down to pick up the newspaper, the whiteness of her breasts became exposed and he inhaled again. On the top of one breast, there was either a small tattoo or a bruise; he couldn't tell which from that distance. He watched her go back inside with the newspaper and close the doors behind her.

Will stayed for another few minutes waiting for his breathing to slow before driving home.

Clouds gathered throughout the afternoon, the temperature fell, and by evening, a steady rain was falling. Will sat under the awning on his back patio with a bottle of beer, watching it. He wondered if it was raining in Northern California where his ex-wife and her lover were. It had been several months since the divorce had been finalized and he wondered if they'd since gotten married.

Then he wondered where Tessa was and what she was doing. He wondered if anything significant had transpired since her journal entry. Perhaps she had ended things with the man. He hoped so, but something about the way she'd appeared on her front step made that seem unlikely. He thought again how ironic the proximity of their houses was: only a few miles, a handful of turns.

He sat forward suddenly, set the bottle down at his feet, and walked to his car. The streets were mostly empty in the rain on his way over to her house. He parked in the same spot and looked out his driver-side window again. The curtains were opened. Through the ringlets of water on his windowpane, he saw Tessa standing in the light of a stand-up lamp. She was dressed in the same robe and was gesturing emphatically with her fist at a man in front of her. The man was tall and well-built, handsome. He was bald, with a dark stubble of beard, and he stood very still listening to her. When her gesturing stopped, he waited a moment, then grasped one of her arms just below the elbow and led her out of the room.

Will sat for several minutes looking at her empty living room before getting out of the car. He pulled the back of his jacket up over his head against the rain and trotted across the street. His steps were silent on her lawn as he approached the side of her house where the two of them had gone. He stopped a few feet away from a window that was cracked open. From inside, he heard her moan, "No, no, no." But it was impossible to tell what emotion was behind those words.

When the room became silent, he returned to his car. He sat staring at his hands on the steering wheel and the rain pouring down the windshield. He watched a car's headlights approach through the rain. Once it had passed him, he started his own car and left.

Will wasn't looking for Tessa when he came upon her next the following Tuesday afternoon. He was getting produce at a farmer's market that was about to close. He saw her at the stall next to where he was buying oranges, searching through bins that held bouquets of flowers. She wore tight jeans and a red fleece pullover. Up close, she looked even more striking and hard. He watched her push a stray strand of hair behind an ear and settle on two bouquets of tall sunflowers. After she paid, he followed a ways behind her as she walked to the end of the market and into a parking lot. She moved unhurriedly, with a gentle ease, and her hips swung in a manner that seemed almost arrogant. When she got to her car, she stood the flowers on the passenger seat and drove away. He watched the tops of the nodding flowers disappear into traffic.

At home, Will wandered through the empty rooms, lifting things that his ex-wife had left and replacing them: a clock on the mantel, a book, a hairbrush, a music box he'd given her, a snow globe from a ski trip they'd taken together. Afterwards, he lay down on the patio pavers and watched the sky dim towards evening. For a while, crickets called. At one point, sprinklers started in a neighbor's yard. A dog barked nearby. But, mostly it stayed quiet until the sky had darkened completely.

Will waited until Saturday to next drive over to Tessa's house. He passed her driveway where she knelt beside her car, fiddling with a jack. He parked several houses away and watched her in his rearview mirror as she tried unsuccessfully to raise the rear side of her car.

Will waited until the jack had tipped over on her third try before he got out, walked slowly up the sidewalk to her, and stopped at her driveway.

As evenly as he could, he said, "Need a hand?"

She turned where she knelt and looked at him. The morning was unusually hot and there was a line of sweat down the back of her T-shirt. Her cheeks were flushed from exertion. She regarded him with no expression for a long moment before finally replying, "All right. I can't seem to do it."

He knelt beside her, notched the jack, and used it to raise the back of the car. She put the flat tire in her trunk once he'd replaced it with the spare, and then did the same with the jack and crowbar when he'd finished with them. They stood looking at each other in the bright sunlight behind the car. There was a thin mustache of perspiration over her top lip. To be doing something, he brushed his hands together until she said, "Thank you."

"No problem."

Her head was cocked and she seemed to be studying him, squinting in the white light. She said, "Can I give you something for your trouble? Money? Something to drink?"

"Water would be good."

She nodded and he followed her up onto the front step. He stopped there when she went inside and waited in the shade, watching the bit of screen flap in the hot breeze. Through the door, he could see the sunflowers in a vase on a small table in the foyer, black-and-white photos of desert landscapes on the walls, the spot in the living room where she had been standing with the man. He heard a refrigerator door open and close and then her footsteps returned. She came out onto the step next to him, the screen door yawning closed behind her, and handed him a plastic bottle of cold water. As she did, he noticed cuts or scratch marks on the insides of both her wrists. If she saw him looking at them, she gave no reaction.

Will unscrewed the bottle and took a swallow. She folded her arms across her chest and seemed to be studying him again. In the shade, he saw crow's feet at the corners of her eyes and a crooked worry line above her nose.

"So," she said, "do you live around here?"

"Not far."

She nodded. "I don't think I've seen you before."

"No."

She nodded some more.

He took another swallow of water and pointed the bottle towards the screen door. "I can fix that for you, too, if you have a screwdriver. Wouldn't take long."

She glanced at the torn screen, and then gave a small, sad smile. "Okay, sure."

She disappeared back inside and returned with two sizes of screwdrivers. He handed her the bottle and took the smaller of the two. She watched as he pried loose a small section of the rubber piping at the corner of the screen's frame, pressed the flap back into place, and refitted the piping over it. It took less than a minute.

She said, "Now I really need to do something to repay you."

He took a breath, then said quickly, "I'd be pleased if you'd have coffee or a drink with me sometime." He shrugged. "If you're available. Or if you want to. No worries if you don't."

She hadn't stopped studying him, but something had softened slightly in her face. "All right," she said. "No harm in that, I suppose. When? Where?"

He suggested later that afternoon at a restaurant bar nearby.

"I won't be able to stay long," she told him. "I have dinner plans."

"That's fine." He nodded. "All right, then. I'll see you later."

She gave the same small, troubled smile. He walked back out onto the sidewalk and continued up it in the direction he'd been going. He walked in a manner that he hoped seemed natural, but he put his hand over his chest when he came to the corner and whispered, "Stop."

He walked around the block and back to his car. When he got into it, he glanced in the rearview mirror again before he drove off. She was no longer on the front step; except for her car, the driveway was empty, and there was no one in her yard. So, he supposed she was inside filling her time however she filled it.

She was already seated at a small table in the bar when he arrived, one empty martini glass in front of her along with another nearly full one. She sipped from the glass as she watched him approach and sit down across from her.

"Hello," she said and took another sip from her drink.

Her expression remained flat. She wore a simple blue dress and a light cardigan sweater of a similar shade buttoned almost to the collar. She'd put on a little lipstick, but no additional makeup.

Will said, "You look nice."

The same smile as earlier creased her lips as she sipped. A waiter came up to their table. Will pointed to Tessa's glass and said, "The same."

"Two," she told the waiter and sipped again.

Their table was next to an open window. The small breeze had cooled a bit, but it was still unseasonably mild. Will looked around the place, which wasn't crowded. It was quiet, just the occasional murmur of voices and slide of glasses.

"So," he said. "Tell me a little about yourself."

She looked at him evenly for a moment, then said, "What do you want to know?"

"Well, how about work?"

"I work, yes."

Will nodded and smiled. "At what?"

"I tend bar." She sipped. "You?"

He shrugged. "Something boring with software."

"Oh," she said. "Okay."

The waiter brought their drinks and set them down. Tessa took a last sip from the one she was holding and he took both of her empty glasses away.

Will raised his drink towards her and said, "To your health."

She gave the same smile, clinked his glass with hers, sipped, and looked out the window.

"How about for fun," he said. "What do enjoy doing for fun, Tessa?"

She turned quickly, her eyebrows knitting. "How did you know my name?"

A flush spread over him. "Your license plate. On your car this morning."

"Oh," she said again, the harshness in her features easing. "I suppose I should ask you yours."

"Will."

"Will. That's nice. Simple, solid. A name for someone who would help a woman with a flat tire or a broken screen."

Will shrugged and smiled again. "So," he said. "For fun?"

She shrugged in return and said, "I'm not a big one for fun."

"Why is that?"

She took another sip and regarded him in the same studying manner as before. "I'm not actually sure," she said. "I wish I knew."

"Everyone deserves some fun," Will said. "Something that makes them happy."

Her eyes filled with a sort of desperation that was quickly replaced by something like mirthful disdain. She looked as if she might laugh. Instead, she swallowed off the rest of her drink and stood up. "Well, thanks," she said. "I have to go. Those dinner plans."

"Wow." Will straightened in his chair. "So quick?"

She extended her hand and he shook it. He fought an impulse to kiss the back of it. Then, she was gone. Through the window, he watched the back of her go off up the street and around the corner. He turned and looked at her chair and her glass with its toothpick of wet olives. His breathing quickened as a slow anger rose inside of him. He sat rubbing his chin for several more minutes, then put money on the table, and left.

Will drove to her house and pulled into his usual spot. Tessa was just getting out of her car in her open garage. The same man from the other night sat on her front step. His head was down, his shoulders shook, his hands were clasped between his knees. As she approached him, he looked up at her, his cheeks wet with tears. She stopped in front of him, took his head in one hand, and brought his face against her stomach. He reached his arms around her buttocks. She put her other hand on top of his shoulder and looked off above him at something in the distance.

Evening had begun to fall. An old woman walking a dog on a leash came up the sidewalk. She passed Tessa's house and had rounded the corner before the man rose. Tessa took his hand in hers and they went inside. The doors closed behind them. The curtains on the living room were drawn. Purple was mixed with blue in the inky sky above the roof of her house.

Will sat while several cars passed by him and the streetlights had blinked on, then drove home. When he got there, he went through the motions of making himself a sandwich and a glass of milk for dinner. He sat at the table under the ceiling lamp, eating slowly. He hadn't removed his ex-wife's table setting next to him since the morning she left: a placemat, plate, silverware on a paper napkin, an empty juice glass, an empty coffee cup. She'd come into the kitchen that morning while he was making their breakfast carrying a suitcase with a look in her eyes not unlike the one in Tessa's when he'd said she deserved happiness. He didn't know why he left the table setting there; he'd tried to take it away several times, but couldn't make himself do it. He set his unfinished sandwich on his plate and looked at the setting, and then outside through the window at the darkness.

Over the next few days, Will felt untethered. He started to drive to Tessa's house several times, but didn't make it there until the following Saturday morning. He didn't know why he was there or what he would do, but he parked and looked across the street. Her car wasn't in the driveway and her garage door was closed. The living room curtains were still shut. He took a deep breath, blew it out, got out of the car, and crossed the street.

He found three newspapers still in their wraps when he came up on her front step. He rang the doorbell. When no one answered after several moments, he rang it again. Silence followed, so he knocked loudly, then peered through the small window on the front door: the sunflowers and table in the foyer were gone, no photos hung on the wall, the living room was empty of furniture. Something fell inside of him.

Will turned around on the front step. The old woman was coming up the sidewalk with her dog. When she drew even with him, he asked, "Do you know what happened to the woman who lived here?"

The old woman stopped and regarded him. She shrugged and said, "Saw a moving truck in front a few days ago. That's all."

"Do you know where she went?"

She shook her head. "We didn't really know each other. Only spoke a few times. Was she a friend of yours?"

"Not really, no."

The old woman nodded while her dog nosed at the dry grass at the edge of the lawn. "She liked to pet my dog. Said she had one when she was little. It was the only time I saw her smile." The old woman paused. "She always seemed a little lost to me, a little forlorn. I hope she's all right."

Will nodded. "Me, too."

"Well, then."

She gave a tug on the dog's leash and Will watched them continue their way up the sidewalk. As hard as he tried, he couldn't imagine Tessa as a young girl with a dog. And during his marriage, he couldn't imagine his wife ever leaving him. But, both had happened.

He sat down on the front step. He thought about the man who had been sitting there the week before and the exchange he'd seen. He thought about Tessa's move; it could mean nothing or everything and anything in between. There was no way to tell or ever know. He thought about his ex-wife, about her new life and their old one, and how they would never cross again. He thought about the things people said and did and those they kept to themselves. He thought about how little he understood about either.

Notes from the Hanged Woman
Kirby Wright

Face it, we're wind
From womb to the blue prom.

Remember me licking
Cream off your belly?

I swing soft breasts
Over the bones of the forgotten.

Creation and death
Harbor in beds.

Can't recall why I hate you
Yet want to keep the investment.

I take my wrinkles to bed,
Hoping to dream young.

Cold tea on the nightstand.
Cat between my legs.

Listen for the cracked dawn.
The riot is close.

Gamblers Hands
Carl "Papa" Palmer

*M*y ring and middle fingers are the same length, he points out, showing me his open, cupped palm. *I have the hand of a gambler. You have it, too.*

This knowledge passes from father to son at the kitchen table as he picks up the four dice and hands me a pair.

His lesson begins:

Opposite sides of each cube add up to seven: one and six, two and five, three and four. Always curl a six with your little finger, picking up a die cube in his right hand holding the six on top.

Sliding a six guarantees you'll never crap out, explaining an instant loss occurs with the roll of two or three, losing both your bet and turn to shoot. *With the solid six all you need is a one or five for the instant win, Seven Come Eleven or another six called Boxcars which pays the shooter double.*

Shake the other dice in your hand against the held six, sounds like you're rattling them both for luck. This won't work at the casino where you have to toss the dice against the wall, but on a pool table at the bar you'll make more than running the rack.

Practice until you can win when you want, but show the others you can be an occasional good loser, too. Win just often enough where it looks like luck and use their money to graciously buy that last round of beer.

It takes a lot of talent to be a winner, not just with dice.

The Hidden Elsies
Andy Bailey

At most, you'll get two opportunities in life, Giselle's father told her when he decided he'd had enough of the Army, though he spoke with that slippery drawl so the word came out *opportunas*. Two opportunas to be someone amazing, or do something remarkable, and you had to be willing to capture those opportunas and wrestle them into gasping submission in order to create the life you wanted.

This was after the sixth base in five years; the family hadn't even fully unpacked in Tacoma before he was transferred to Jacksonville, North Carolina. Being one of few land mine technicians came with perks, like higher pay and rank, but it also meant that he was in demand all over the country, especially since action in the Middle East had picked up and those primitive bastards scattered IEDs like Johnny Appleseed.

This is my second one, he'd said. His old high school sweetheart lived in Jacksonville, having just divorced her drill instructor husband, and damned if he wasn't going to woo her like he did on prom night 1979. Only catch: She refused to be with anyone still enlisted. Living with a drill instructor could turn a person like that. After their mother had died, and their bitchy stepmother left with the gap-toothed warrant officer at Fort Hood, it'd just been Dad and the three girls, and despite her best efforts as a matriarch, Giselle knew her father and sisters needed someone in charge who didn't have to budget time for geometry homework. *Gonna take this opportuna to be happy*, he said. Missed the last one, and Satan and Santa Claus together couldn't stop him this time.

"Goddamn, I thought California was supposed to be warm all the time." Ryder had decided not to go full drag, owing to the jet lag and the unfamiliar surroundings, instead donning a baggy gray hoodie and thick beanie that covered her shaved head. The sun was out, but its sickly yellow light faltered somewhere over the ocean, pushed by the salty breeze that made Giselle shiver in her flouncy sundress.

"Sun's brighter, at least. Purer," Giselle responded, though she wasn't sure this was true. They'd come to the Venice Boardwalk first, but first implied a second, which implied an entire itinerary that they did not have. The trip to LA was supposed to be a getaway from New York and the *NStreet Bois and all the drama that had erupted.

Ryder had convinced Giselle not to set a plan, to just allow the days to present themselves with no expectation. No expectation, no disappointment.

A guy hawking rap CDs offered a discman to Ryder for a sample listen. "Yo, homeboy, check this shit out. Dopest beats on the beach."

Ryder waved him off, affecting her stage voice as they continued moving. "Nah, man, we're tight."

He began walking backwards to keep up. "Come on, Dude, maybe for your girlfriend?" He stopped, took a deep look into Ryder's face, then broke into a laugh. "Oh, shit, ya'll are both bitches. My bad." He continued laughing as they moved on.

"No problem, asshole," Giselle called over her shoulder. Always easier for her to talk shit, since she wasn't trying to pass. She'd hung out with her bandmates enough to pick up on the looks, the whispers, the outright prejudice that before she would've sworn didn't exist.

Ryder shot her something between a scowl and a smile, a nervous hand running over her neck in a way that only could've been called girlish, though she would've hated that. "Way to scare him off, tough guy."

Giselle nodded. "That's what I'm here for."

Late afternoon on a Tuesday and the crowd was sparse—sunburnt Midwestern tourists as easy to spot as the beached-out locals. "What should we do?" Giselle asked, to fill up the silence. Ryder would get like this, moody and introspective, filling perhaps too well her role as the Chris Kirkpatrick/A.J. McLean "weird one." Of course, the unspoken connection between those two was that Ryder was the "ugly one" too, which perhaps led to the brooding, which led to more strange behavior, all a vicious cycle of mimicry that had lately devolved the *NStreet Bois into near-dissolution.

They approached the fenced-off pen that enclosed Muscle Beach. A few roided lifters hovered over each other, screaming supportive and vaguely sexual comments as they tried to swell their already-freakish bodies to grotesque extremes. Ryder leaned over the fence to watch, nodding for Giselle to join her.

"Now these guys ..." Ryder stared at the pectoral slabs of a bald guy doing bar dips "... they're the shit."

"They're gross."

"That's right, you like skinny little bitch boys, don't you?"

"And you like skinny little bitch girls, don't you?"

Neither laughed. Giselle felt the few seconds of silence swell with importance and she braced herself for whatever Ryder was preparing to say.

"Piper Perabo."

"What?"

Ryder nodded. "Piper Perabo."

"You mean that chick from *Coyote Ugly*? I hate that bitch."

Ryder ignored her, watching intently as an old guy loaded up a barbell with enough plates to make it sag, clearly delusional about his lifting ability. "That's when I knew. I mean, I had known, for a while, but couldn't really admit it. But I saw that movie, saw her, and that's when I *knew* knew." Ryder smiled, first one of the day, and ran her hand across the fence's rail, closer to Giselle's. She'd been subtly trying to grab Giselle's hand throughout the walk, fingers grazing across palm, but Giselle had pretended not to notice, pulling away to inspect novelty sunglasses or the two-headed snake outside the freakshow. But now, watching lonely men in the weight pen preen and flex for the attention of anonymous bystanders, the heavy reality pressing down that no matter what happened, they would not be going back to the same place they had left, she reached over and took Ryder's hand.

Ryder didn't look, didn't smile, instead accepted Giselle's palm, and squeezed.

Her father's first opportuna had been as a young man. The director of the Arkansas Boys' Choir had made a special trip over from Little Rock to Anthonyville at the behest of Mr. Pierson, the school's music teacher, who insisted that Giselle's father Jack had a voice that would rip evil from souls of the most impenitent men. He liked singing, sure, but he'd only joined the school choir after there weren't enough interested boys to field a town baseball team. The first day, when Mr. Pierson had them run through *Zip-A-Dee-Doo-Dah* as a warmup, he stopped the class mid-song and made Jack keep singing, then made a face like he had to go to the bathroom and rushed out.

When Jack told Grandma Ditty about the audition, set for Tuesday after school, she started to cry. Then she stayed up late tailoring his older brother's work shirt until it fit Jack just right, shining bright white like an invulnerable force field.

A defective force field, turns out, that couldn't stop the stares and taunts from his classmates when he showed up for school on Tuesday dressed like he just came from church. The force field failed completely when Doby Jones pushed him down at recess, called him a sissy, then threw a glop of mud onto the white shirt. Did he think he was better than everybody, just because he could sing stupid songs like a girl?

And Jack should have said something, used his voice and told him to get lost, maybe even fought back; he was about the same size as Doby, and everybody would've been on his side.

But he lost it. He opened his mouth, staring up at Doby's blackened grin, and tried to force out a word, a sound, anything. The voice had gone. Doby was right: he wasn't special, he did sing like a girl. At the audition after school he sang flat, out of tune, squeezing his eyes together so he wouldn't have to see the boredom on the choir director's face or the horror on Mr. Pierson's.

He lied and told Grandma Ditty he did great, the director wanted him on the choir, and she cried again and called everyone in the family. But after a week or two, when there were no permission slips to sign, no practices to take him to, she stopped asking about upcoming concerts, stopped bragging to neighbors. Never asked him about it, but would cut out articles about the boys' choir from the local paper: performances in Washington D.C., Disneyland, even a trip to Hawaii. Sounded like a made-up place, an alien land in the comic books he kept hidden under his mattress. *Hawaii.*

So, when the time came, he joined the military, in hopes of traveling to the same places as the Arkansas Boys' Choir. Even marked a pocket-sized map, red dots for the choir's stops, blue for his. As the dots drifted farther and farther apart, never creating purple, the blue sticking to large, open areas in the middle of the map while the red hugged the coast, that was when he took up smoking, to deaden the voice. To keep it from escaping, to ensure that no one ever encouraged him to try out for the Army Chorus. He never sang along with the radio, never at church, just nodded solemnly during the *Star-Spangled Banner* at ballgames, then fired up a cigarette immediately after.

They stayed like that, holding hands and watching the lifters, until Giselle shivered and brought her arms around herself, walking away before Ryder could offer a hug.

"Want to go to a bar or something?" Ryder asked as she caught up. "Have a beer, watch the sunset, talk shit about people walking by? Or we could score pot from one of the hippies?"

Giselle shook her head, wanting to keep moving. Staying in one place too long would allow her thoughts to settle, which would allow her feelings to creep in behind. With the rush of renting a car and finding the hotel and the distractions of the boardwalk, she hadn't really had time to process the flight and their conversation.

Notes of—again—girlish desperation in Ryder's voice. "Or we could … I don't know, get ice cream? Go shopping? Tell me what you want, I'll do it."

That was what they needed, she realized. To talk. Right now. She was only making things worse by letting everything linger, by not talking. By holding Ryder's hand. It was supposed to have been a relaxing trip to get out of the city and forget her breakup with Stoner Steve—though break-up wasn't the right term, "agonizingly slow fizzle-out" was much better—but after the plane ride, after Ryder's weird silence when she should've been laughing at the fat guy across the aisle farting in his sleep, after Ryder looked at her and opened her mouth and changed the tenor of the trip and the *NStreet Bois and the whole fucking world at once. After all that, Giselle knew she wouldn't be doing any relaxing.

"Let's head toward the ocean," she said and cut from the boardwalk across the bike path and onto the impossibly wide beach, the salty smell of the ocean much stronger than the faint crack of the waves that exploded in the distance.

Giselle's first opportuna was the interview at *Teen Vogue*. The position was an online content editor, which, as far as she could tell, consisted of either writing scathing critiques of celebrity outfits or oversharing personal advice on how to handle body hair. It wasn't interviews with George Clooney in Lake Como, but it was a start. More than that, it was perfect. Her thesis advisor at NC State had set it up through an old friend, giving her one of those rare big-city chances that didn't happen to unconnected military brats, and most certainly not unconnected military brats from NC State.

But when she'd walked up to the Condé Nast building, having fought through the crowd at Times Square and nearly rumpling the business skirt she'd ironed three times the night before, she got hit with the shakes. Real, jewelry-jingling, DT-quality shakes like she imagined Uncle Joe got every morning before he drove his pickup off the Rock Creek Bridge. She'd only been in New York two weeks and still hadn't felt that rush, the drunkenness of possibility that was supposed to hit recent transplants as they stepped out of a SoHo wine bar or 24-hour Burmese restaurant and face the limitless night. Instead, she'd barely left the closet-sized room she rented in an Alphabet City walkup, except for food runs to the same sandwich shop or trips down the hall to the shared bathroom that always seemed to have someone crying on the other side of the door.

Be a trooper, she told herself, balling her hands into knotty fists as she entered. She stepped into the elevator. As the door shushed closed, a hand shot inside followed by a wispy blonde girl who—after pushing the same 38 button that Giselle had just pushed and offering a scared, apologetic smile to everyone in the elevator—Giselle knew would be interviewing for the same position. The girl picked at the hem of her skirt and spoke quietly to herself, either giving herself a pep-talk or practicing answers to an unseen questioner. When a cell phone went off in the elevator, blaring "Party in the USA," the girl jumped, then hurriedly dove into her leather tote to silence it, spilling her keys in the process.

Giselle picked them up off the floor and handed them back to the effusively thankful girl, but not before spying the Columbia University keychain.

And that was it, all Giselle needed—not a condescending look or question about her educational background, but a keychain. She quickly played the interviews out in her head, herself straight-laced and conscientious, answering all the questions politely and to the best of her ability, doing an admirable job of hiding just how badly she wanted it; while this other girl would stumble in and effortlessly give entertaining answers peppered with a well-timed curse word, remaining so charmingly flustered that she'd even forget to give the list of references, which probably included a man with a last name that graced a building on that same street and her writing sample, which would be a breezy piece on the pros and cons of sexting while in a long-distance relationship.

Giselle's sample was her thesis, which discussed the ambiguity of narrator reliability in *Canterbury Tales*.

When the elevator stopped a few floors below the *Teen Vogue* offices, she got out and walked the stairs all the way back down. She spent the rest of the afternoon in an East Village coffee shop, obsessively checking her phone with a mix of disappointment and relief when it didn't ring. *Teen Vogue*, as well as the professor who set up the interview, never called back. Eventually she found a job as a receptionist at a global banking company with a lot of consonants in its name, stumbled into singing with the *NStreet Bois when they cornered her at a Chelsea karaoke bar after hearing her rendition of "Do Ya Think I'm Sexy" and felt something that could have, if she kept busy enough, passed for happiness.

But still, the thought stayed with her. What chance did she have in life, if her deepest dream could be thwarted by a keychain?

It was just them on the beach. They sat on a sandy decline that hid civilization from view, a few ugly birds dipping in the wind above them. She hadn't meant to pick such a dramatic spot. Though it was certainly a better setting than in the cramped confines of United's economy class.

"I love you too," she'd told Ryder as they hung somewhere over the Midwest. But then Ryder gave a shrug and nodded like a teacher encouraging a reluctant student, and Giselle finally caught on right as the plane shuddered, the air currents that bore the jet now struggling to support the extra weight of Ryder's proclamation.

"I mean, why did you think I was coming with you to LA?" Ryder asked now, letting a handful of sand sift through her fingers.

"I don't know. To be my friend? Console me after the breakup?"

"You are my friend." Ryder looked out to sea, not meeting Giselle's gaze. "I just ... how can you not know? Why do you think Chance and I broke up?"

"I thought you disagreed about the harmonies for *I Want You Back*." Off Ryder's scoff, she added, "Not just that, but ..." A breeze carried off the rest of the sentence.

How could she not know? The inside jokes, the constant hugs—neither had that kind of connection with anyone else in the group, even Chance and Ryder when they were dating. All the late nights at her apartment, chugging wine, talking shit, falling asleep in the same bed afterwards. She spent more time with Ryder than with Stoner Steve, even at the height of their relationship. Had she truly not suspected, or was she so flattered by the attention that she convinced herself that it was harmless, that Ryder was just flirting, that things would pass like they always had?

"But I'm straight," Giselle blurted. Wasn't she? There was that sleepover with Lisi Crooks in tenth grade, and the college party where everyone was on E, but those had been harmless experimentations. She'd never felt a deep pull.

Except.

Two weeks ago. Chance had pulled her into a bathroom stall at The Duplex after a show, both of them high on adrenaline and vodka. Two standing ovations and an encore, and the manager had immediately booked them for the next month. Giselle had always thought Chance hated her, ever since she'd taken all of Chance's solos on the closing medley. But before she knew what was happening, their hands came alive, awakened and kneading an unfamiliar language into each other's bodies. She tingled like she never had with a man.

Did Ryder know about it? Was that why she and Chance had broken up? There were too many webs; Giselle felt snarled, so she stood up, waving her arms to free herself from the tangles. Ryder stood, too, but kept looking out towards the ocean as the sun neared the horizon, finally slicing below the cloud line into a smog-enhanced bloodshot glow. Somewhere down the beach a drum circle had fired up, carrying tribal beats toward them in heartbeat rhythm.

"I'm not asking for your hand in marriage or anything," Ryder said. "I just can't pretend anymore. And if this fucks everything up, I'm sorry. I'll leave the group. Spent most of my life hiding, and I'm too old to keep doing it now."

Ryder met her eyes. There was depth there. A big, pillowy depth, perhaps enough cushion to break a fall with minimal damage. Another breeze swelled up and Giselle hugged herself. She saw Ryder hold back from reaching out.

Giselle nodded. "Didn't you mention something about a drink?"

A smile in return. She let Ryder lead this time, turning her back on the sunset as she picked her way over the sand, back toward humanity.

It was misty, which it never was, not that late into summer, and this made the night air heavier than Jack had ever felt it in Jacksonville. Appropriate. The extra weight would help. They'd done a preliminary sweep that afternoon, and he had watched as the sappers-in-training cleared three acres of dummies. Didn't take them as long as it should have; he'd scattered the dummies carelessly across the field, giving no more than a perfunctory effort. Had to make it look like he still cared, up until he was discharged, but like hell he was going to work any harder than he had to. Nearly thirty years of service and he still had jerkoffs like Major Greene busting his ass for inappropriate spacing and clustering. Like the Army really cared about any of the fuckwits it employed as minesweepers.

Jack's boot prints, their roundness, their humanness, clashed against the mechanized lines and angles of the tank tracks that lurched out of the night at him. The mist dampened sound, too; the crunch of his boots the only violation of the silence. He felt like the only human in the county, the state even, a post-apocalyptic survivor wending his way around blast craters and metallic rubble. The MPs had already done their rounds so it was just him, tromping toward the wire fence that separated the dummy field from the live one.

Maybe he should've hesitated more before he punched in the gate code and swung the gate outward. But it would've only been a symbolic delay; he knew exactly what he had to do. Had since he first saw Lena again. She had tears in her eyes when she told him she still thought about him, had through all four marriages, and now wanted nothing more than to wrap him in her arms and succumb to that soul-searing adolescent love that had never been fully dampened.

But I can't marry an Army man, she'd cried. Not anymore.

They'd scattered Elsies throughout the northern part of the field. Anti-personnel mines, Elsies were designed to punch a hole in the foot, maybe take out a few toes. Very low fatality rate. The brass wanted to test the new Buffalo armored vehicles before shipping them to the Middle East. Testing Elsies was a waste of time, Jack had told them, as the insurgents weren't using them and they couldn't even scratch the Buffalos' armor, but every contingency must be accounted for, he was instructed. No matter how asinine.

He passed through the gate and into the virgin field. The sweep wasn't until the next day, so the ground lay untrampled, inviting, as he unlaced his boots and stepped onto the cold dirt. He flexed his toes, digging them deep as he could, creating ten little trenches. But there was nowhere for them to hide.

He didn't tell Lena what his plan to get discharged was, but she was with him when he stole Mr. Shaw's Buick out of the faculty parking lot senior year: she knew what he was capable of. He'd given her a small kiss, just enough to quell the fire, and then she pursed her lips and cocked her head and told him to come back for more when it was done.

Sergeant Lowe had laid the Elsies, so Jack would have to stumble around to find one. He closed his eyes, whispered Lena's name, and jumped far as he could into the field. The smack of his landing shivered through his legs and up his spine as he held his breath.

Nothing.

He bent deep, then leapt again, then again, each time saying her name louder until shouting, the thump of each landing bringing him closer to the hidden Elsies, closer to Lena, closer to love.

Wake Dance

Ellen Girardeau Kempler

My idea of heaven is an open house
where the dearly departed arrive
in dancing shoes, carrying hot dishes,
hard liquor, deadly desserts—the works.

We welcome them back with hugs & kisses,
as if they were merely gone a minute,
questions & tears strictly forbidden—
wherever they were, we'll never ask.

It's not polite. Besides, we've got the Dead
at 27 Club tuning up downstairs, & Mozart
up here, powdering his wig. Frankly,
it's hard to choose between the floors.

Narrow River

B. R. Lewis

Leland turned the key in the ignition. The old green pickup sputtered, clearing its throat as it rumbled to life. Once the engine would run without his foot on the gas pedal, he stepped out of the truck's cab, crunching the brittle, frosted dirt beneath his boots. The sky was clear, a hopeful sign that the early chill would burn off with the rising sun. He scraped his windshield as the truck warmed up, then cleared the side windows and mirrors.

Before he climbed back in, Leland cracked the canopy's rear window. Inside he saw the lumber and tools precisely where he had left them after visiting True Value during lunch on Friday. Only the long beams had been moved. He had cut those into the required lengths the night before, trying to keep this project from lasting all weekend.

Back in the cab, Leland warmed his hands over the dashboard heater and sipped directly from his thermos of coffee. The fan belt squealed as he put the truck in gear and headed east on Highway 14 toward the county line.

Arnold had called him at the garage on Tuesday, in a near religious fervor about violations of tribal rights and the treaty of 1855. His cousin was furious because the platform below Husum Falls was gone. The lumber had already washed down the White Salmon, on its way to the Columbia. *I hope it jams the lock*, Arnold barked through the receiver, *or sinks some goddamn Mayflower's wind board*. Leland sighed, twisting the phone cord between his fingers. He'd built the platform a month ago and it had yet to be used.

He didn't ask if there was any evidence that the stand had been torn down. Arnold's slurred speech, peppered with curses, made his suspicions clear. The river was high, but the spring flows weren't wild enough to wash out the platform. And Leland didn't need his cousin to point out the obvious suspect. *Everybody knows Josh Sanders pulled it down*. The owner of White Water Adventures had organized the coalition of rafting companies. He had vowed to reverse the decision to allow the platforms by any means.

Leland told his cousin not to worry, that he would repair the structure as soon as he could. He couldn't make it out to the falls until Saturday. The garage was backed up with work and he couldn't afford to close it up during the week. Husum was forty-five minutes from the garage, and building the walkway wasn't an after-dinner project. Not that the delay made any difference, since there were no fish anyway.

During the course of the week, several other cousins called, along with his grandfather, Norman. They called the garage so often that Leland started to wonder if he would ever get any work done. He was already tense. Susan had been on him all week, convinced he was dragging out repairs so he could overcharge for her Volvo's front end work. The sales rep was always impatient; that's why she took a corner too tight and clipped a short retaining wall. Actually, he wasn't charging enough. She glared and tapped her high heels each time he asked her to wait while he answered the phone.

The calls continued when he was home, eating his frozen dinners in front of the TV. His grandfather was particularly livid. He was going to drive the 120 miles from his HUD home in Wapato and rebuild the platform himself. All he needed was someone to load up the camper. *Just let me stay out there a few nights with my shotgun, Lee, and we'll see if anyone has the balls to tear it down.* Leland barely managed to talk him down, reassuring him that he had everything under control.

Highway 14 snaked along the northern walls of the Columbia River Gorge, occasionally dipping down to the river. On the shotgun seat of the cab sat a red truck-stop baseball cap, embroidered with the image of a peace pipe and *Native Pride* in block letters across the bill. Norman had given it to him. The old man had jumped at the chance to volunteer his grandson to build the traditional fishing platform on the White Salmon River. Norman was a member of the tribal fishing council, and claimed that their family had always fished this stretch of water, before the Condit Dam. When Leland initially tried to decline the honor, the eighty-four-year-old said he would build it himself, rather than tell the council his own kin refused.

Leland relented, choosing not to call his bluff. Norman immediately brightened, produced the hat, and shoved it down on Leland's short hair. That was the only time he had worn it. Beyond the cap, there would be no compensation, other than the gratitude of the tribe. He saw little honor in the task, or even why it was necessary to build a platform on a river that hadn't seen a single salmon for more than a hundred years. With no fish ladder, the dam had blocked the salmon from the river and they had wisely gone elsewhere to spawn. But he was the only son of Norman's oldest son, and God only knew where his father was these days. So the responsibility fell to him.

Leland crossed into Klickitat County and turned left onto the

Highway 141 spur. The wide gray expanse of the Columbia in the predawn light vanished from the rearview mirror after the first bend. The two-lane road wound its way toward the town of Husum. A rusted sign pointed to the Northwestern Lake boat ramp; someone had forgotten that the lake was gone, drained away when the dam was breached. Near the Falls Bridge, cafes, bed and breakfasts, and the storefronts of commercial rafting companies lined one side of the street. A nowhere place, he thought, where people lived to be disconnected.

The White Salmon cut down through the foothills of Mount Adams, in the borderland between the eastern and western sides of the state. Husum Falls was a transitional place, where pine and fir trees mingled. He had camped in these woods one fall, stalking elk and eating government surplus cheese sandwiches with Norman. His father was already gone by then, and he looked so much like Norman's son that Leland's mother decided she couldn't stand to look at him anymore. Without hesitation, his grandfather had taken him.

Over the years, Norman had taken him camping and hunting, trying to teach him self-reliance, stressing the importance of remembering where you came from. During one of those trips, in the woods near Husum, Leland and Norman had brought down a five-point bull elk. As they set about skinning and preparing the meat, the game warden pulled up. He wanted to see their tags. They didn't have any; Norman saw no reason to buy a license for a right he was already guaranteed. *All the usual and accustomed places,* his grandfather had intoned, looking the officer in the eye. But the warden persisted, *This ain't the rez.* The meat was impounded for the warden's freezer. They loaded up the camper and went home early, his grandfather cussing all the way back to Wapato about how the cowboys always win.

Leland parked at the gravel turnaround near the bridge and heard the dull roar of the falls. A gravel path led to stone stairs to the right bank of the river. The trail was not meant for him. It was built for conservative kayakers who wished to launch below the falls, bank fishermen, and hot-blooded teenagers in need of a make-out spot. The county would not have constructed a trail to allow easy reclamation of native rights along the narrow river. Nevertheless, he appreciated not having to traverse a slope of crumbling dirt and loose rock to reach the stony edge. Leland unloaded his planks, tools, and a small cooler.

The sun was barely beginning to peek over the hills. Whoever dismantled the platform had been thorough; not a single support beam remained in place. The drop frothed with white water and filled the air with a fine mist as the river spilled over clean granite and basalt, unimpeded by his handiwork. Husum Falls was divided into three chutes by a pair of rounded boulders that protruded from the river like worn canine teeth. The platform had to span fifteen feet, from the shore to the outside corner of the center chute, over where the water pooled below the falls.

A cool northeastern breeze funneled down the riverbed and sent a shiver through Leland's body as he began to construct the scaffolding. He buried the ends of two sturdy beams on either side of a broad flat stone near the water. Ashes from the fireplace hearth and dirt from his ancestral home—the flowerbed near Norman's front steps—were mixed with the soil that covered the ends, as his grandfather instructed. Fortunately, he still had some of the potting soil from the last time he'd buried the beams. Next, stilt legs were fitted precisely into natural notches in the stones. A series of angled crossbeams between these legs would reinforce the structure's frame. The platform would be held to the shore by the tension of its parts.

By midmorning the canyon warmed under the early spring sun. Leland removed his jacket. He wiped the sweat from his brow and stretched his stiff lower back. His work had gone largely undisturbed; only a few cars passed, and a handful of joggers rattled the bridge deck over his left shoulder. He knelt on the uneven surface of the rock and began to nail the planks to the frame. The sound of his hammer echoed off the foothills, creating a steady rhythm in the still morning air.

These platforms were common on the Columbia, under the Bridge of the Gods in Stevenson, where he lived and worked. In his youth, Norman told him how Coyote had taught his people how to harvest the salmon. Starving, cunning Coyote exploited the sex drive of the fish, as the Coho and Chinook blindly marched up the river to spawn. The trickster created waterfalls and forced the salmon to the surface. Then he constructed the first platform out of poplar and willow branches and slung a net below its frame. Coyote built a fire in the shade of a great pine tree and waited for the net to fill with his slippery prey. And he taught these methods to the Yakama.

The story always reminded Leland of the Husum Falls hunting trip, Norman sitting near the campfire, the blaze reflected in his thick glasses. He had a somber look on his face as he watched the flames dance. *These are our lands Lee,* he said, using his medicine man's voice; *they are a part of you.*

Leland had never fished with a net. Nor did he think it was likely he ever would. His grandfather had described the process of hoisting the heavy, fish-filled seines as backbreaking. Between the slight shifting of the platform and the slickness of the planks, a man was just as likely to drown as to catch enough fish for his whole family. The last time Leland had fished, he had been a child standing on the shores of the Yakima River with Norman. A single rod and reel between them. They caught nothing and picked up some burgers on the way home.

Even if you managed to catch a net full of salmon, what the hell would you do with all those fish? Leland pictured his lazy Klickitat cousins, hung over, sitting on their fat asses in lawn chairs surrounded by coolers. He couldn't imagine them pulling a loaded net out of the water. They peddled salmon to whites at the in-lieu site above Bonneville Dam or in the Charcoal Burger parking lot. Their jeans were stained with guts, and their shirts permanently reeked of fish oil. Chief Char-O-kee, the restaurant's cartoon Indian mascot, smiled over them with his twin braids, red headband with a single feather at the back, potbelly protruding above his loincloth.

On command, a fish hawker would play noble shaman for the tourists, especially if he also sold dreamcatchers and other trinkets. Hands stretched toward heaven, he would tell garbled tales of the gods, especially Tyhee Saghalie, and his two sons, Pahto and Wy'east. All people were united by a land bridge across the river, before the jealous sons forced their father to destroy the connection. To Leland, the fish peddlers possessed a self-righteous air, as if impressing whites with folklore somehow preserved their cultural heritage. He would rather break his back in the garage than listen to any white call him chief or Tonto, or try to barter for fresh salmon with whiskey.

By noon the platform protruded five feet over the water. Leland felt the morning's work in his knees. Over his left shoulder, the low murmur of congregating voices floated toward him from the steel bridge. Husum Falls was the highlight of White Salmon rafting trips. Leland knew that most tour companies stopped just above the falls, to let off those who were too young or too timid to take the plunge. These groups walked to the bridge downstream to watch the others drop. One such group, probably one of the first of the season, gathered around a perky guide. Leland stopped hammering and listened to her bubbly voice:

"The White Salmon River was named for the pale color of salmon carcasses after the fish have spawned. It's estimated that nearly twenty-five thousand people raft Husum Falls each year, making it the largest commercially run falls in the United States. Oh, on your right you can see a member of the Yakama Tribe constructing a traditional fishing platform. Since the removal of the Condit Dam three years ago, eight miles downstream, the tribe remains hopeful that the namesake fish of the river will return."

The group broke into individual conversations that blended with the steady babbling of the river. Some wondered aloud why Leland didn't wear his hair long. Others admired the falls but complained of the chill. A few tried to get Leland to wave, as if he were part of the tour. The platform creaked and shifted slightly beneath him as he crawled forward, assembling the structure section by section. He needed to place another set of legs in the water, to brace the overhang where the netman would stand.

As he stood to retrieve a post from the shore, Leland noticed the crowd's silence. He turned and saw the red raft poised, ready to plummet down the center chute. The raft wobbled, unbalanced by an odd number of passengers, as it made its descent. From the top of the chute it slid over the smooth rock tongue of Husum Falls, then dropped the first three feet. The guides shouted commands to the amateur rafters dressed in bright yellow life vests and gray helmets. Frantically, the oars on the right stabbed the choppy waters, in a desperate attempt to shove off concealed boulders and maneuver toward the left bank. The raft took the last drop and landed against the pool with a loud slap, audible even over the constant noise of the water.

Leland visualized the placement of the constructed platform. The vessel would have clipped the outside corner. He wondered if that contact would have been enough to flip the raft as it spun around under the influence of the unbalanced load. The helmets and life jackets all bore the insignia of the outfitter, White Water Adventures. The white circular logo included the name written in slanted letters encompassed by a cresting wave. The raft's master looked back at the unfinished platform; Leland could tell he was also imagining the completed structure. On the bridge, the crowd cheered and waved before being led toward the rendezvous point downstream.

How many careless boaters would be flipped by his platform? How many rubber rafts ruined? Once the brace legs were set, the near chute, popular with kayakers, would be completely blocked. Leland knew this deck wasn't the only obstruction he had been charged to build. Eventually, smaller platforms would hug the shore, allowing better access for hand nets near the outer edges of the pool. The final stage was a short platform, to the shallow rapids above the drop.

Leland hadn't attended the hearings about the multiple-use plan for Husum Falls. He knew their tension and bitterness second hand, from phone calls with relatives back on the reservation, conversations with customers, or newspaper stories. The Yakama delegation had refuted pie charts and economic bottom lines by invoking the ghosts of Celilo and ancient treaties. Finally, after months of debate, the Department of Fish and Wildlife reluctantly admitted that the tribe had priority. Even when white governments declared they had no reason to interfere, Norman scoffed, reminding his grandson that had never stopped them before. Since Leland didn't fish, he had only a passing interest in the issue.

Then Norman showed up in Stevenson to personally deliver the good news: Their family would resume its traditional role as the keepers of the White Salmon platforms. They sat in Leland's living room, his grandfather grinning, with a cooler between his legs and an eagle feather in his wide-brimmed hat. Gray braids hung down on either side of his weathered face. The cooler held a jar of salmon eggs, two dead jack salmon, dirt from the flowerbed, and braided sage grass.

As he leveled the next section of frame, Leland remembered again how he tried to talk his way out of the job. The platform wasn't important to the family. This river, the salmon, if they ever returned, mattered little to their people. Freeways had replaced the game trail, and the tribe was focused on roadside casinos, not salmon runs. Norman insisted that winning money from moss eaters, although satisfying, didn't make you any less subjugated. *Those who forsake the old ways are fools who have sold their own hearts.* The old ways meant little to Leland; he lived in a doublewide and bought his food from a grocery store. Still the old man persisted: *The salmon are a part of us.*

The sun grew closer to the foothills toward the west, and Leland knelt at the edge. He shoved the post into pale green water a half foot out, struggling against the current to keep it in place. When he felt the soft silt and gravel of the river bottom give beneath the timber's butt, he slowly rose, placing his boot on the post to hold it steady. With his boot, he angled the post back to the nearest crossbeam. Then Leland took the sledge and drove the post deeper into the river bottom. Once it was stable, he secured the leg to the frame with a pair of long nails and repeated the process on the other side of the brace. With the legs in place, he resumed planking the expanding deck.

In the distance, Leland heard the shrill cry of a train's whistle. He looked up from his work, wondering whether the train was headed east or west. A car paused on the bridge, idling, before it continued toward Highway 14. Probably someone checking Leland's progress before reporting back to Hood River. He watched the road until the car was out of sight.

Throughout the afternoon and into the early evening, he pieced together the sections, framing and then overlaying the slats. When the deck was complete, there was nothing left to build but the overhead scaffolding. The single archway, placed near the center of the walkway, would be used to help hoist the large nets from the water.

With the platform rebuilt, Leland walked back to the shore. The boards creaked beneath his boots. He retrieved a salmon carcass and a jar of eggs from the small cooler, and the sage grass braid and lighter from his jacket pocket. The sun was low in the sky, painting the horizon pink. Leland stretched his back, arms and legs; this wasn't how he'd hoped to spend the weekend. Normally he would sleep in, before going downtown to the Snag to have a few beers, play darts, and watch the Blazers game.

The carcass he freed in the shallow waters near the shore, an offering to show his people's respect for the salmon. It drifted quietly over the gravel. He lit the sage grass and slowly waved the smoldering braid over the structure. Norman claimed the smoke would purify and protect the wood from bad spirits. Leland grimaced, noting that the smoke hadn't saved the first platform from destruction earlier that week. Once the sacred smoke had touched every inch, the braid was left to smolder on the rocks at the entrance. The small fire would invite Coyote to sate his ferocious appetite from the narrow river.

He noticed someone was watching the ceremony from the end of the bridge, but Leland was running out of daylight. He smeared the little red eggs on the legs where they met the water, to encourage the salmon to remember these forsaken spawning grounds. The final step of the ceremony, Norman told his grandson, was the most important. In the scaffolding, Leland hung a willow branch to recognize Coyote's ingenuity and his generosity in teaching the people to fish. He secured the branch with the twine traditionally used to make nets.

Leland didn't believe in these charms, but now he wouldn't have to lie when Norman asked if he had anointed the platform. He surveyed his work from the shore. The old man had provided the spiritual instructions, but the deck and dock construction were based on modern techniques researched at the Stevenson Public Library. He stepped roughly on the center of the walkway and bounced. Shockwaves passed through the planks, reverberating out to the pale green pool, and quickly disappearing in the swirling current. Barring a flash flood or human intervention, the platform should last through fishing season.

The sunlight was fading and the temperature began to drop. Leland returned his canvas jacket to his shoulders. Suddenly he felt hungry; he had consumed little beyond coffee and beef jerky and his stomach rumbled and churned like the water below the falls. Although no one was standing by the bridge, Leland sensed someone nearby.

He picked up a few spare beams and headed up the embankment. At the turnaround, a silver Subaru Forester with Oregon plates was pulled up close to the bridge. The roof rack held a kayak and a roof box covered with stickers like *My Other Car Is a Mountain Bike* and *Rafters Do It In The Water*. Leland thought of the stickers on Norman's truck: *Insured by Smith and Wesson*, *Seattle SuperSonics* and his latest, an Indian Brave holding a sign that read *Unoccupy America*. Leland's truck was free of stickers. There was nothing he wanted to broadcast to the rest of the world. And working in the garage, he'd seen the damage those vinyl vanities could inflict on a paint job.

Inside the car, the driver watched as Leland made several trips to stow the remaining planks. Even in the twilight, he recognized the man behind the wheel. Josh Sanders ran more boats down the White Salmon than any of the other eight outfitters. Leland had never met Sanders, but he'd seen his picture in the paper and on the local stations during the hearings. Although his arguments were not clever, Sanders was aggressive during the hearings: *The Yakama haven't shown any interest in the White Salmon for generations. But now that the river is truly valuable, after we invested in it for decades, they want to cash in. Their platforms will obstruct the river and hurt the local economy. We aren't the ones asking for special treatment. We just want to know why they can't fish from the shore like everybody else?* The crowd behind him had cheered as he flashed a big toothy grin.

Sanders exited his SUV. He had broad oarsman shoulders but stood a good head shorter than Leland. He guessed Sanders was in his mid-twenties but it was hard to tell, as the neatly trimmed brown beard made him look older. As Sanders watched intently, Leland stowed the last of his tools and the cooler and firmly shut the tailgate.

The young entrepreneur continued to stare across the turnaround at Leland and then slowly moved his gaze down toward the water. His eyes were the cold slate gray of a river rock, worn smooth by the water, and possessed a calm, confident quality. Sanders appeared to be waiting, and he was in no hurry to move.

Leland paused halfway to the truck's cab. He wondered if Sanders would have the gall to walk down there and destroy his work after being seen. Sanders continued to wait patiently by the Subaru. Leland felt the urge to knock the self-assured half smile from that smug face. For a moment the two men locked eyes, Sanders's river rocks and Leland's dark as silt. Stubborn pride forced out Leland's most stoic glare. Sanders was daring him to leave the platform unattended.

Leland wished that there was something in the cooler besides raw salmon eggs. Norman's shotgun idea suddenly seemed appealing. He leaned against the hood, arms folded across his chest. "You know," Leland said, "I shot an elk in these woods once. Big old bull, a five-point, stood up in a thicket just a little farther from me than you're standing now. Caught him clean in the chest."

"I don't know what the hell you're talking about," said Sanders.

"Didn't think you would." Leland smiled and entered his pickup, rolled the window down. He turned the key just enough to power the radio and listened to the second half of the basketball game. Above the static and play-by-play, he could hear the crunch of gravel as Sanders paced back and forth. The sun vanished; another train called out from down in the Gorge. Coyotes answered the train with yips of laughter from the foothills. Leland didn't budge.

In the darkness, Sanders slammed the door of the Subaru and peeled out onto the road, spitting gravel in his wake. Leland flipped the key from accessory to start and the old pickup sputtered to life. Go ahead and tear it down, Leland thought as he drove off. He'd rebuild it as many times as it took.

Modeling for the Gods
Fred Rosenblum

A bull moose ruminated on the tender buds
of a fallen white birch I'd felled the day before
Wool-capped and flannelled I
bucked-up green fuel to season and sell
Warm and feed my family in the year to come
and still ... snowflakes fell
thick and wet from the heavy grey veil
of late spring's, precipitous anomaly
A smear of a star, our sun
faint in the flurry
of a nimbostratus, low flame ceiling
Heatless aloft the broken
spears in a drift that sprang with sprouts
of embittered buddings
 — nutty chewables, that I too
though with doubt
and an angst for its difficulty consumed
with cold visibilities of pulmonary escapement
 – frigid respirations, to illustrate
that we were somehow, to some degree
enough akin, so as to begut these
same acrid edibles
A breathtaking demonstration of mandibles
proving, save the obvious lingual and digestive disparities
a connection in this microcosm
beyond the snow globe of our imagination

nonfiction

A Chase to Bear Witness
Alan S. Brown

What the hell am I doing?
My heart pounded like a drum as I scrambled up the side of the mountain. Not a bass drum, but a snare. My binoculars bounced against my chest, and two moisture-wicking layers clung to my skin under the weight of my backpack.

Do I really want to do this?
I'd never chased an animal before with the intent to kill it. While I was straining to get up the hill to intercept the small herd, I was also struggling to come to terms with what I was trying to do. I knew how to shoot and hit a stationary target; the Army had taught me that much. Stopping a walking, beating heart was not the same, physically or psychologically. I had never trained for that.

I raced up the mountainside, hoping to see the moose emerge again from the thick alder brush fifty yards to my left. The alder was all but impassable to me. With the noise I'd make trying to follow their trail through the snarly branches, I'd lose them for sure. No, I had to take a chance and move in the open, negotiating the steep incline full of mossy outcroppings, Velcro-like brush, and boulders bigger than the moose themselves. If they continued up the mountain through the thicket, they might appear in a clearing about two hundred yards up. They might also hear my clambering or see me out in the open and hunker down.

Even though I was doing the hunting, I was acutely aware that moose killed many more Alaskans each year than bears. I was venturing into their territory, threatening to alter their cycle of life. I was following five moose during mating season with only four 30.06-caliber rounds in my Remington—alone. Attempting to take the life of the singular male in the group might have serious consequences.

The hill leveled off, and from my position I saw a clearing above the thicket. If the moose continued moving up the mountain, they would appear in the open space one hundred and fifty yards to my left. That would be my best chance, not that I could shoot straight after the steep sprint-climb. My glasses fogged, and drips of sweat ran down the lenses. I was in no condition to try and drop a bull moose.

Moving up the hill further to try and gain a vantage point, I saw the bull. The cows ambled nearby, but not too close to obscure the view through my riflescope. They were heading up the mountain at the same pace I was, and I knew I might only have a few seconds to take a shot. I threw off my daypack onto a mossy boulder and used it as a rest for my rifle, anything to stabilize my erratic breathing and shaking hands. From there I sighted in the ass-end of the bull. Not a high-percentage angle. I counted a few seconds, trying to calm my breathing, while switching my safety to fire. The bull turned down toward the alder, exposing forty-five degrees of its flank. Sixty degrees would have been better. Ninety degrees would have been perfect. Forty-five was all I was going to get. *Here it goes. One chance.* I exhaled and squeezed the trigger gently, gradually—waiting to be surprised.

CRACK!

The echo pounded the valley. The moose didn't flinch, no reaction at all. He continued his way slowly back down the hill toward the thick brush, following the cows who bolted after the loud rifle report. *Shit. I missed.*

I reluctantly walked to where he stood a minute before. No blood. No indication that I'd hit him. *God, I hope I missed.* I did not want to be responsible for a wounded moose that would either die slowly and painfully or fall victim to prey. What a cruel insult to nature.

I rationalized in my head that the moose would have faltered somehow if I'd hit him. From what I could see, he hadn't moved an inch. He only paused briefly and continued walking toward the safety of the thicket. *Yes, I must have missed.*

I found the trail the cows made fleeing back into the alder. If I could entice the moose back down into the valley where my hunting partners waited, perhaps they could get a shot. I followed the hoof prints, broken branches, and fallen leaves a couple hundred yards down the mountain slope until the trail disappeared in a small clearing—a bald spot amidst the overgrown foliage. The tracks were gone. So was any hope I'd find the group again. I stood there at a loss for what to do next. I could only hope that I'd missed, that I hadn't committed a wasteful, careless sin.

I was out of viable options. Without any blood trail or fresh tracks, my search would be futile. Getting my bearings, I turned to head down the mountainside toward my hunting partners. With a couple hours of daylight left, we could head back to camp and regroup for the next day.

Then I saw him, and he saw me. I had walked nearly fifty steps after resigning my search, and we nearly walked into each other. The moose stood just seventy-five feet in front of me, lightly veiled behind a few thin alders. He walked gingerly, limping from his hind end. Wounded.

He was making his way down the mountain, the same direction as the cows. He hadn't sensed me in the area until I was on him. After taking one more faltering step, he froze and looked at me through the thicket.

CRACK!

The thousand-pound animal sank to his knees, head still up, looking at me. I edged closer, rifle at the ready in case he surged to come after me. I knew I'd hit him in the vital organs, but I had no idea how long it would take him to die.

Moving to within thirty feet but still behind the bush, I aimed again.

CRACK!

He rolled over onto its side, head down. One round left. He was still moving, legs kicking, chest heaving erratically, whether consciously or not I couldn't know. I moved to within ten feet of him, no longer shielded by the brush. I struggled to bear witness as the life drained from his eyes. I thought I was prepared to be a hunter, to locate, stalk, and kill. After doing just that, a surge of conflict overcame my excitement: *I did it!* gave way to *What have I done?* I'd imagined a quick death and a feeling of triumph. Reality felt nothing like that. I was prepared to kill it, but not to watch it die.

CRACK!

My last round exploded into his heart. I stood, empty rifle in hand, waiting for any indication of death—for its sake and for mine. Minutes passed as I watched its motionless body, certain its sacrifice was complete. I should have been excited, elated after the successful, physical hunt. But it wasn't that simple. The animal before me was breathing moments before. And now it was dead. All I could do was stand there staring, wrestling with my feelings. Death was never something I'd faced head-on, even as a soldier in a combat zone. Now standing ten feet from the dead moose, I could not avoid it. I searched for some resolution to the fact that I'd just ended this beautiful creature's life.

When a soldier died in the line of duty, his sacrifice was respected, even revered. There was nothing more honorable than when a soldier died doing what he had pledged to do. We'd mourn his loss and honor his selfless sacrifice, his willingness to give everything. Watching the moose's last breath stirred a similar emotion.

Nature had its own struggles, its own unforgiving fight. When I pulled the trigger, I became part of that cycle, changing the course just like any other unpredictable event at Mother Nature's hand. Had I entered nature's cycle by killing the moose? Or had I merely acted within the cycle I was already a part of?

Our paths crossed for a reason. While I persevered, I was aware it wasn't skill that led me to find him again, wounded. If I'd rolled another number, I may have never come across him, never knowing if I'd hit him in the first place. No, there was something else at play. My notion to turn around after losing the moose tracks in that small clearing was a random gut call. I had resigned myself to the fact that I'd missed, that Mother Nature had just taught me a valuable lesson— her turf, her rules, her wrath, her grace. My second chance was not a coincidence. Being forced to watch his life drain away was also not by chance.

After we hauled the carcass back to camp and hung it up, I was exhausted but couldn't sleep. The events of the hunt replayed over and over again behind my closed eyes: the chase, the shot, the discovery, more shots, dying, death, dissonance. One continuous loop holding my conscience hostage all night. No peace.

There's no trophy on the wall to mark that day, but my memories of the chase, the shots, and the kill endure. I am thankful I could provide such rich, organic sustenance for my family. My kids, eight and five, understand that the meat they ate for the better part of a year came at the hand of my rifle. It matters to them to know where their dinner came from. Just like it matters to my wife and me. Occasionally, my five-year-old son would comment at dinner.

"Daddy, you shot this moose with your gun."

"That's right, buddy. I did."

My kids are curious, but not conflicted. To them, the moose's sacrifice is as nature intended. If only I had such a simple resolution.

I Want to Know the Ending

Penney Knightly

It's not as if I don't want to
because I do.
If you were to ask, I'd say
I'm tired of all the time.
This isn't me wishing I were older
or saying I am done living,
or anything like that.

I just feel like going faster
through the moves a little quicker,
in the movies I'd get a montage,
the way it so romantically portrays,
devoid of struggle and emotion;

I suppose it is impatience,
the unwillingness to wait for inevitability
slow turnover makes me scared.

I like the peace that comes from seeing
an aging woman's body;
she withstands.

Issue 7 Contributors

Andy Bailey, who originally is from Boise, Idaho; teaches English in Los Angeles. His stories have appeared in *Juked*, *Tupelo Quarterly*, and *Cleaver* among others. His website can be found at memyselfandrew.com

Lana Bella is a three-time Pushcart Prize, five-time Best of the Net, and Bettering American Poetry nominee. She is an author of three chapbooks, *Under My Dark* (Crisis Chronicles Press, 2016), *Adagio* (Finishing Line Press, 2016), and *Dear Suki: Letters* (Platypus 2412 Mini Chapbook Series, 2016), has had poetry and fiction featured with over 400 journals, *Acentos Review*, *Comstock Review*, *Expound*, *EVENT*, *Ilanot Review*, *Notre Dame Review*, and *The Lampeter Review*, among others, and work to appear in *Aeolian Harp Anthology, Volume 3*. Lana resides in the US and the coastal town of Nha Trang, Vietnam, where she is a mom of two far-too-clever-frolicsome imps.

Toni La Ree Bennett received a Ph.D. in English from the University of Washington, also studying Italian, editing, and photography. Her work has appeared in *poemmemoirstory*, *Puerto del Sol*, *Hawaii Pacific Review*, *Society of Classical Poets*, and *Seattle Poetry on the Buses*. She has several poems in the anthology *The Muse Strikes Back*. Her photographs have appeared online, in print, and in private collections. She shares her Seattle space with a flock of feisty finches.

Alan S. Brown has lived all over the world the last 20 years while serving in the Army. He and his family embrace Alaska as their heart home, as it is the one place they've lived together the longest (3 whole years). Still on active duty, Alan holds a Master of Arts in English from Colorado State University and currently teaches composition and literature at the U.S. Military Academy at West Point, NY. His work has been featured in *Foliate Oak Literary Journal*, *Fish Food Magazine*, and *Gold Man Review*.

William Cass has had over a hundred short stories appear in a variety of literary magazines and anthologies such as *december*, *Briar Cliff Review*, and *Conium Review*. Recently, he was a finalist in short fiction and novella competitions at *Glimmer Train* and *Black Hill*

Press, received a Pushcart nomination, and won writing contests in Terrain.org and *The Examined Life Journal*. He lives in San Diego, California.

Dah's fourth poetry collection is *The Translator* (Transcendent Zero Press, 2015). His poems have recently appeared in *Straylight Magazine, Otoliths, The Cape Rock, Acumen Journal, Sandy River Review, Indian River Review, The Linnet's Wings*, and *Junto Magazine*. Dah lives in Berkeley, California and is working on the manuscript for his seventh poetry book. http://www.dahlusion.wordpress.com/

Alissa DeLaFuente grew up in Mount Vernon, Washington, traversed the desert in search of herself (with little luck) at the University of Arizona, and earned her Master of Fine Arts in Creative Writing from Western Washington University in the somewhat sleepy small city of Bellingham. She writes fiction and nonfiction and currently works a full-time gig in Student Services in the same city. This is her first major print publication.

Richard Dokey's story collection, "The Loneliness Cafe," has just been released by Adelaide Books, New York. His stories have won awards and prizes, have been cited in Best American Short Stories, Best of the West and have been nominated for the Pushcart Prize. "Pale Morning Dun," his collection, published by University of Missouri Press, was nominated for the American Book Award.

Anara Guard is a fiction writer and poet who lives in Sacramento. She has attended Bread Loaf Writers Workshop and the Community of Writers at Squaw Valley in fiction. Her collection of short stories, *Remedies for Hunger* (New Wind Publishing) received four stars from the Chicago Book Review. She has just completed her first novel. Follow her on Facebook at www.facebook.com/AnaraGuardAuthor or at www.anaraguard.com

Teresa H. Janssen holds an M.A. in Linguistics from the University of Washington. Her nonfiction has received the Norman Mailer/ NCTE award, Pacific Northwest Writers prize, and a Travelers' Tales Solas Gold award, and has appeared in *Anchor, Obra/Artifact*, and *Tidepools*. She lives on the Olympic Peninsula where she tends her orchard, teaches, and is at work on a memoir about one extraordinary year of her life. More about her writing can be found at www. teresahjanssen.com.

Ellen Girardeau Kempler's first chapbook, "Thirty Views of a Changing World: Haiku + Photos," will be published this year by Finishing Line Press. Her poems have appeared in *Rising Phoenix Review*, *Cargo Literary*, *Orbis*, *Spectrum*, and others. Individual poems received Ireland's Blackwater International Poetry Prize (2016); honorable mention in the Tom Howard/Margaret Reid Poetry Contest (2016); and multiple awards in her Laguna Beach, California, hometown. She believes in poetry's power to move people to action.

Robert Hoffman received a dual MFA from NILA at Whidbey Island, Washington. He's the author and publisher of the "15 Poem" series, with a fifth book with a release date by winter 2017, "15 Road Trip Poems and a Total Eclipse." He is published in *Panoply*, *Cordite Review*, and *sharkreef.com*. Robert lives in Lakewood, California with his childhood sweetheart of nearly 40 years.

Penney Knightly is a survivor of sexual abuse; themes about that are often found in her work. Her poetry has appeared in *Dead King*, *Ink in Thirds*, *Eunoia Review*, *Cleaver Magazine*, and elsewhere. She lives with her family on a sailboat in the San Francisco Bay, where she writes and makes art. She tweets @penneyknightly and shares on her blog http://penneyknightly.com.

Georg Koszulinski has been making films and videos since 1999. His award-winning works have been presented at hundreds of colleges, universities, and film festivals around the world. Fandor recently released his *Florida Trilogy* (2007-14) and his experimental film essay series focused on the Pacific Northwest, *Frontier Journals #1-8* (2013-15). His most recent documentary project, *White Ravens: A Legacy of Resistance*, focuses on the Haida Nation and the cultural resurgence taking place on their islands of Haida Gwaii.

B. R. Lewis graduated from Western Washington University and earned his MFA from Eastern Washington University. He served as an editor for both *Willow Springs* and *Sundog Lit*. He currently lives in Roseburg, OR where he teaches at Umpqua Community College.

Ken Mootz's work has been published by multiple outlets, including *Empty Sink Publishing*, *Weirdiary*, and *Todd Suck Review*. In his spare time, he likes rooting for the Dodgers, trying not to stress out about work, and playing laser with his cat, Baxter. Ken and his wife live in Huntington Beach, California.

Simar Malhotra is a junior at Stanford University studying English and Public Policy. Born and raised in New Delhi, India, Simar writes about characters faced with situations idiosyncratic of the typical Indian society. She started her career as a writer at the age of 16 and is the winner of the Bucock/Guerard Fiction Prize at Stanford. When Simar's not toiling away at her desk working on fiction, she works towards building more inclusive economies through service.

Toti O'Brien is the Italian Accordionist with the Irish Last Name. She was born in Rome then moved to Los Angeles, where she makes a living as a self-employed artist, performing musician and professional dancer. Her work has most recently appeared in *Calamus*, *Dying Dahlia*, *Circleshow*, and *Fire Poetry*.

Carl "Papa" Palmer of Old Mill Road in Ridgeway, VA now lives in University Place, WA. He is retired military, retired FAA and now just plain retired without wristwatch, alarm clock, or Facebook friend. Carl, president of The Tacoma Writers Club and Franciscan Hospice volunteer, is a Pushcart Prize and Micro Award nominee. MOTTO: Long Weekends Forever

Jennifer Pullen received her PhD from Ohio University. She originally hails from the wilds of Washington State but now holds a position as an Assistant Professor of Creative Writing at Ohio Northern University. "Those Who Stayed" is from her manuscript of short fiction. Her fiction and poetry have appeared in journals and anthologies including: *Cleaver*, *Gravel*, *Blink-Ink*, *Phantom Drift Limited*, *Clockhouse*, and *Prick of the Spindle*.

Fred Rosenblum is a poet living with his wife in San Diego, California. His poems have appeared in publications throughout the U.S. and Canada. Fred's debut collection, *Hollow Tin Jingles*, was released in 2014 by Main Street Rag and his second collection, *Vietnumb*, currently rests in the queue of Fomite Press—scheduled for release in the fall of this year.

Laura Schulkind is an attorney by day, where she is entrusted with others' stories. Through poetry she tells her own. Her chapbook, *Lost in Tall Grass*, was released by Finishing Line Press in May 2014. Her writing has also appeared in numerous journals, and can be found on her website: www.lauraschulkind.com, along with musings on why "lawyer-poet" isn't an oxymoron.

Claire Scott is an award-winning poet who has been nominated twice for the Pushcart Prize. Her work has been accepted by the *Atlanta Review, Bellevue Literary Review, Enizagam,* and *Healing Muse* among others. Claire is the author of *Waiting to be Called* and the co-author of *Unfolding in Light: A Sisters' Journey in Photography and Poetry.*

Eileen Shields received her MFA from UCR's low rez program. Recent publications include: *The Los Angeles Review, Rumpus, The Toast, Slice, Word Riot,* and *The Nervous Breakdown.* She is also the screenwriter of *The Amaranth,* a feature film currently in post-production. She lives in Manhattan Beach, CA with her spouse and her dog. Links to her work can be found at eileenshieldswriter.com

Patty Somlo most recent books are *The First to Disappear* (Spuyten Duyvil), a Finalist in the 2016 International Book Awards and the 2016 Best Book Awards, and *Even When Trapped Behind Clouds: A Memoir of Quiet Grace* (WiDo Publishing), a Finalist in the 2016-17 Reader Views Literary Awards. She received an Honorable Mention in Fiction in the 2017 Women's National Book Association Contest and had an essay selected as Notable for Best American Essays 2014.

Kathleen Tyler's publications include *The Secret Box* from Mayapple Press and *My Florida* from Backwaters Press. Her poems have appeared in numerous journals including *Quiddity, Women Write Resistance Anthology, The Rattling Wall* (Pen/USA), *Visions International, Runes, Solo, Poetry Motel, Margie, Seems, Cider Press Review,* and others. Her manuscript, *Open the Window and Drown,* was a finalist in the BrightHorse Books Contest. It is forthcoming from Kelsay Books.

Kirby Wright's third play was performed at the Manhattan Rep's 2017 Non-Fest. He won the screenplay writing award at the 2017 Video Nasty Film Festival in Seattle and also the Gold Fox Award at the 2017 Calcutta International Film Festival for his treatment of an animated series.

Bob Zahniser lives in Oregon and loves it there. He's been a member of the "Easy Writers" critique group in McMinnville, Oregon for over 10 years. His work has appeared in *Belleville Park Pages, Walk Write Up, Perceptions, Skylight 47,* the *Ottawa Arts Review,* and elsewhere.

www.ingramcontent.com/pod-product-compliance
Lightning Source LLC
Chambersburg PA
CBHW031843170626
46807CB00004B/1604